MW00461315

SINGLE, PREGNANT, AND PREACHING

(REVISED EDITION)

AUTHOR- Melvina L. Carpenter

© Copyright 2007 Melvina Brown,
Revised edition Melvina Carpenter
All rights reserved. No part of this
publication may be reproduced, stored in
a retrieval
system, or transmitted, in any form or by
any means, electronic, mechanical,
photocopying,
recording, or otherwise, without the
written prior permission of the author.

CONTENTS

Memories Oh Memories………………………………

Rayne on Me!………………………………………

Trouble Cometh……………………………………
…..

What happened to Everybody?………………………

Words of Motivation and Encouragement from the Author…

SINGLE, PREGNANT AND PREACHING

She felt his arms encircling her widening waist. "Come on baby don't be like that," Tony replied pleadingly. She felt his body calling out to her. She tried to move his hands off of her but she was not physically strong enough. He had a grip on her. "I miss you," he said. Before she knew it he spun her around to face him and kissed her so tenderly she thought she was floating. It took everything in her to gain the will to resist him. Relentlessly, she pulled away. "Tony, I said stop." She looked more determined than she felt. On the inside she was doing a cartwheel for the mere fact that she was standing up to him. She'd never denied him before so he was in shock. However, deep down inside, she almost felt like it was turning him on. Never the less, she had to stay focused. "What's wrong, you don't miss me Emerald? You don't love me anymore," Tony asked with a sadden look on his face as he allowed her to step back from his grasp?

"Here's the deal Tony, I have a lot on my plate and dealing with you is not what I have a taste for right now." "Yeah, well what exactly do you have a taste for," he asked while walking towards her again? Emerald had to think just to respond because her body wanted to leap into his arms and beckon him to take her right there. She backed into the pantry door and had nowhere to go. "I want you so bad right now Emerald. You look so sexy being pregnant." He hovered over her with his tall frame and she felt like she was going to suffocate. Her flesh and her spirit were in a literal fight. It was up to her which one would win.

THANK YOU

I give undying thanks to my Lord and Savior Jesus Christ for giving me the strength, wisdom, knowledge and understanding to write this book. Everyday I love you more and more.

To my husband, Deacon Willie M. Carpenter, III, you are my gift from God! You are my fantasy man and proof that fairytales can come true. Thank you for loving my daughters as your very own and supporting me with the revisions of this book. Thank you for being my biggest supporter as I am yours as well. I love you today and always.

To my inspiration, my reason for living, my push when I feel like throwing in the towel, my children, Genesis and Corinthia. I pray that your husbands will love you as Christ loves the church and gave his very life for it. Genesis, remember, you're my heart and daddy's love, Corinthia, you're my promised child, my ray of sunshine. I love you both. Azian, Keylowrae, and Blair, thank you for being a part of my life and sharing your Dad with me and the girls. You bring me joy! Our five children represent grace. I love you all! Also, to my nephew,

(adopted son), Carlique Scott, I love you
son.

To my parents, Pastor Melvin and Evang.
Kathy Wright, (*True Light Healing and
Deliverance Ministries, Goose Creek, SC*)
thank you for always believing in me and for
instilling in me that I really can do all things
through Christ that strengthens me. To
Mom, the most beautiful, best dressed even
on a bad day, most creative designer and
decorator, most extravagant cook in the
world. You are so anointed that you can
turn a one-bedroom shack into a palace! To
my Dad, the first priest that I knew of, that
set the example of what a Godly man should
be, your smile illuminates my heart, your
wisdom speaks to me during difficult times.
You are a man of integrity and valor and just
as handsome as you want to be!

Thank you both for the pedestal that you put
me on. You had vision so that I wouldn't
perish. Hey, I'm a king's kid; I am of a
royal priesthood, a peculiar person and a
chosen generation. Thank you for your
integrity, your prayers, your talks and yes
daddy, thanks for the spankings too. It made
me who I am today, a wife, mother, Elder,
Prophetess, author, singer, educated,
daughter of yours. God couldn't have given
me better parents. You're my world!

To my siblings, Shonda, Melvin Jr., Carey and DeAngelo, you all are my world. Thanks for the laughs, for the tears, for the arguments and everything else that I can't mention. Melvin, thanks for having my back. How would I have made it through college if it wasn't for you watching my children? Carey keep on playing that keyboard boy---you are awesome and even moreso- ANOINTED!! Shonda, my world is great because you exist in it. I Love you sis. What an awesome mother you are to your daughter. DeAngelo, you'll always be my baby! Keep God first, and watch great things happen for you. To all of my siblings, thanks for being you! To my nieces and nephews, Serenity, Chloe, Micah, Conner, Carey Jr, yall keep this Auntie going and I love you! Chante Wright, you are an asset to our family (a clown just like us) and we love you!!!!

I have no living grandparents, but to my Aunt Beatrice Robinson, You are my world. Thanks for being there. Also special thanks to with Uncle Robert & Aunt Carriebell Jamison and Uncle Willis & Aunt Rose Jamison, Pastor Janie & Min Ike Grant, Uncle Joseph & Aunt Margaret Gathers, Uncle Alonzo & Aunt Michelle Wright, Uncle Benjamin Alston & Ms. Debra Brown, Aunt Pearl Nesbitt, I love you.

To my dear friends, Scherrie Nick (my cuz),
My Aunt, Betty Smith, Uncle Kelvin &
Aunt Angel Wright, Uncle David Wright,
Elder Lakeisha Allen, Ashely Fyall,
Minister Camilla Martin, Prophetess Buffie
(Senelvia) McIver, Elder Tara Butler,
Keisha Denmark-Wigfall, Elder Odessa
Purdy, (thanks for watching my children
while I attended college.), Michelle Bell and
Pas./Prophetess Priscilla Brantley (*New
Covenant Deliverance Min., Columbia, SC*)
Missionary Patrice McCormick, Missionary
Laverne Skipper, Elder Tyrone & Min.
Anita Shaw, and Deacon William &
Claudette Hannah, Elder Demestress
Williams, thanks for encouraging and
praying me through!

Apostle Norma Y. and Prophet Thomas E.
Gray, thank you for speaking life into my
spirit. (*Global Dominion, Rock Hill, SC*)

Apostle James and Lady Linda Deas, thank
you for believing in me. (*Simply Unique
Int'l Min., Bronx, NY*)

Apostle Helen and Deacon Flash Kinloch,
thank you for leading me to Christ and
loving me unconditionally. (*God's Way
Healing and Worship Ctr. Mt. Pleasant, SC*)

To the congregation of True Light Healing
& Deliverance Ministries, I love you and

thank you for all of your prayers and support.

Last but not least, to the man that looked at me and saw the Melvina that God created, Pastor Ezekial Wright, (New Covenant Life Church, Huger, SC) thank you for not throwing me away when the people told you to. I love you man of God. As promised, no matter where I go in life, I will never forget you!

If I forgot to mention your name, please don't take it personally. Know with in your heart that I love you all. Thank you, thank you and thank you.

DEDICATED

To the memory of

The Late Alfred Alston & Bertha Mae Alston

And

The Late James Wright & Sadie Wright

Part 1

MEMORIES
OH
MEMORIES
....

CHAPTER 1

It was a chilly evening in Charleston, SC.
The fall weather was in full effect. Emerald
Sinclair had just gotten in from work and
was exhausted. The blue and white cotton
suite that she wore to work today seemed to
be shrinking because she was definitely not
gaining any weight. She had worn under
one hundred and fifteen pounds for the past
five years. She tried everything to gain
weight but nothing seemed to work.

She dropped her black leather coat in the
middle of the floor along with her bags and
proceeded to the kitchen. Did her roommate
cook anything for dinner? "Of course not,"
she thought. That was always a rare
occasion. Her roommate, Flora worked as a
preschool teacher and she was always tired.
When Flora was home, she was in her room
resting or talking on the telephone.

Emerald decided to order Chinese. Sesame
chicken and shrimp fried rice sounded
divine. She called the restaurant to have it
delivered. When the call was over she
leaned against her refrigerator and
reminisced to herself about her last
encounter with Tony, her long lost
boyfriend. It has now been two to three
weeks since she had seen or heard from

Tony and she was seriously contemplating ending their so-called relationship.

The last time they were together was just what her body needed (and craved now actually)! But it was also what her spirit rejected. However, in this case, her flesh won. His 6' 7"and 190 lbs of all dark chocolate covering and filling her body in every way was exhilarating. His frame was complete with no body parts falling short! His dark eyes seemed to look right into her soul and give into her every desire of him.

It was so close to the holidays and depression was creeping in. She wanted to be loved, she wanted to be married and she wanted him. Every time they made love, it proceeded with a day of repentance for Emerald. She knew that it was wrong but how could she resist him? He was almost perfect. He was a picture of glorified erotica himself with the lines and charisma to match. She always tried to tell him no when he approached her but after a while the no's became compromised. "You can spend the night but we're not having sex." "I just don't want to be alone tonight," she'd say. He'd spend the night and after 1am, hands and mouths roamed. They felt and touched on everything on the other person's body that could be felt or touched. It was exciting to Emerald and almost addictive.

How do you resist the cold air being on your
face and his warm body on your back?
How do you say no to his moist, thick lips,
nibbling at the nape of your neck, kissing
your ear, while caressing your thighs and
telling you how sexy you are? As he does
this he is allowing you to know that he
needs to be one with you! It was very hard
for Emerald to resist and daily, the struggle
was becoming more intense.

No one really knew about her secret life.
People knew that she was seeing someone
but not to the extent that she 'saw' him.
Tony became the one thing that brought
Emerald out of her prayer closet.

They went to church together on occasion
and Tony seemed to enjoy it. Afterwards
however, he questioned and or criticized
every part of it. That annoyed Emerald
royally but she figured that if he kept
coming, God would eventually save him.
Following church, they would go out for
dinner or have dinner with her family. Then
they would go back to her apartment for
more of his service instead of God's service.

What drove her to him? She knew that it
was wrong but other than food, water and
life he was next on the list. She felt
protected with him around. Her 5'4" frame

against him made her feel like she was a princess and he was her night and shining armor. But little did Emerald know, her world would come crashing down right before her very eyes.

CHAPTER 2

Just then her doorbell rang and interrupted her thoughts. There he was, standing there with a smug look on his face that Emerald wanted to slap off and then kiss the pain away. "Hey," he said as he pushed his way through the door. Emerald's appetite just dismantled itself. It was only two weeks before her initial sermon and she was already on edge. The last thing that she needed was to see him. But oh how her body ached for him. However, tonight, her spirit man would win the battle.

They were dating for about seven months when he proposed. She was just elated. He was so attentive when they first met. He always complimented her, bought her things, took her around his friends and family, but lately he's been in this whole new world. "What do you want Tony," Emerald asked with an attitude? "What do you mean what do I want? I came by to see you but if you're going to act like that then I can leave." Emerald was fuming on the inside. It had been two weeks since she spoke to him. She called him and got no answer. She left messages but he didn't return her calls. She blew his pager up but still got no response. Now he's acting like all is well. Well it's not! "Let's go for a ride," Tony offered, "I need to talk to you." He sighed, kissed her on the cheek and her body melted. But she played it off by wiping her cheeks where he kissed her. He shook his head and opened the door. She agreed to the ride and into his Dodge Ram pickup truck they went.

They rode around looking at the homes with Christmas lights already up and waiting for the major holiday. "So, how have you been," Tony asked Emerald? "Fine I guess, how about you?" "I've been alright," Tony said with a shrug. "I haven't been feeling so well lately though. I've been vomiting and having headaches like crazy." "Good," thought Emerald, "you deserve it." "Speaking of," Tony said, jolting Emerald out of her thoughts, "when was the last time you saw your friend?" "What friend," Emerald asked with an annoyed look on her face and in her tone? "Your monthly friend," Tony said with sarcasm in his voice. "I don't know, two months ago," Emerald said carelessly. "And you don't see anything wrong with that," Tony asked? Emerald was always irregular so missing her monthly was nothing that alarmed her. However, recently she's been off and on with her birth control but she had done that before. "Everything is alright," she thought to herself. She looked at Tony with exhaustion spread across her face. "You need to take a pregnancy test Emerald," Tony said in a demanding tone that did not sit well with Emerald at all. "I'm not taking any pregnancy tests! If I was pregnant don't you think I would know? You must be sick because of those hootchie mama's you've been with that's kept you away from me for the past two weeks." "Whatever," Tony said, "we're going to go get a test right now." Emerald didn't object. Tony didn't deny Emerald's accusation of him cheating on her and that infuriated her even more. Feeling defeated, she rested her head on the window and they rode in silence to the store. He went in to purchase the test but Emerald remained in the truck.

"I couldn't be pregnant," she thought. "The devil is a liar. There is no way that I could be pregnant." Quickly, Tony returned with the test in hand and they went back to her apartment.

As soon as they got there she went directly to the bathroom, opened the test and followed the directions. She set the timer and nervously awaited the results. While waiting, she looked in the mirror at her reflection. "There is absolutely no way that I am pregnant. My parents will kill me. I am twenty-four years old, in my own house, but they will kill me." The timer sounding brought her mind back from her dreary thoughts.

There it was, two lines on the EPT stick. Emerald's hands shook as she held it. "I'm not pregnant," she yelled! "Thank you Jesus. Oh thank you, thank you, thank you. Ooh that was so close. God I promise I will hold out for my husband. Thank you Jesus!" She did a dance around the bathroom while singing and screaming, "I'm not pregnant." Tony rushed in. "What's going on? What are the results," he asked excitedly? "I'm not pregnant," she said bouncing around in an I told you so position. He looked at the stick, then at the box and back at her. "Yes you are," he said. "One line means negative and two lines mean positive. You have two lines here. You are pregnant!"

He dropped the box on the sink and went into the bedroom. "I don't want anymore children Emerald. I can barely take care of the one that I have now." Emerald felt a hot wave rush to her heart and thought that her life would end right there. One because he was telling her that she was pregnant and two because he was flipping on her when she needed him the most. Her palms were sweaty and her breathing short. She felt like she'd be passed out on the floor in approximately three seconds.

She was pregnant. "But this couldn't be," she thought. "Not me, I'm preaching my first sermon in two weeks." She paced the bathroom floor while thinking.

"What will the church members think? What will my parents say? What will the members of the community think? I'm the eldest of five children. What will my siblings say? I'm supposed to be setting an example for them. I'm the praise and worship leader at my church. What will the teen girls in my church say once I start showing? Everyone on my job knows about my initial sermon. Will they lose respect for me?"

She was in a daze. Her world was tumbling even the more before her. At that moment she wondered if the pieces would ever be picked up again.

CHAPTER 3

She lazily went to Flora's room and showed her the test, with tears running down her face. She felt like she was drowning. Her roommate ended the telephone conversation that she was having. She looked at Emerald, nervously laughed and asked, "Whose test is this?" Emerald pointed to herself. Flora fell back on the bed with tears in her eyes as well. Emerald walked out of the room and into her own bedroom. Tony was lying across the bed when she entered. He sat up and started again about not wanting a baby. "What do you want me to do Tony, have an abortion? I'm not having an abortion Tony, that's out of the question. You can cancel that," Emerald said full of anger and determination. A girl that Tony had a one-night stand with had an abortion for him right before he met Emerald. She was not going to do that for him or any other man.

Blatantly Tony said to Emerald, "I think we need some time apart." He rose from the bed and stood. What Emerald couldn't believe was, not only was he not being responsible for this baby but also he was trying to walk out on her. She had supported him when he had nothing. She was always there for him and now he was abandoning her. "Well be gone," she thought. Emerald was always independent. She didn't depend on anyone for anything. That's how her parents raised her. She was working since the age of sixteen. Sometimes she worked two jobs while going to school. She was now working at a promising cell phone company as a customer service representative with a pretty nice salary plus commission. Emerald was not about to rely on this trifling, no job, workers compensation having, two days in a row clothes wearing, little boy. She took the engagement ring that he gave her and gave it back to him. She asked him to leave her and her home. She would raise this child, love and care for it even if she had to do it all by herself. As he walked out of her bedroom door and out of her apartment she knew that he was walking out of her bed and her life forever.

CHAPTER 4

Emerald cried herself to sleep. Before she knew it the alarm was going off and it was time for her to get up for work. "There is absolutely no way that I can go into work today," she thought. Emerald's job was fairly easy and stress free but it also allowed her plenty of thinking time. She knew that she'd be thinking of this all day and did not feel like the questions from her co-workers concerning her silence. Emerald was always known as the clown of any group so if she was quiet, then she was either upset about something or extremely tired. Emerald was tired but it was more emotional than physical.

Her entire life, she was known as the preacher's daughter. Lil' miss goody two shoes, is what they called her behind her back. She tried to be perfect. She loved the

Lord but men were her weakness. She wasn't whorish but she had a few long-term relationships that had damaged her and here was one more notch of pain on her belt.

She was tired! She'd started college and recently quit because she was too tired after work to sit in a classroom for four hours. That was a big mistake and she was realizing it. Now she has a baby in her belly. "Who will it look like? Will it be a boy or a girl? What will I name it? Will my parents help me? Will my Dad ever speak to me again? What if it's mentally challenged?" The questions rode her mind until she finally remembered that she still needed to call out to work and make a Dr.'s appointment to confirm the pregnancy and schedule her monthly visits.

In the meantime, her friend Pamela was a registered nurse and could give her a test on the down low. Pamela tried to keep Emerald and Flora in check. Often times she brought condoms to them and questioned them about their birth control methods. She made sure to talk to them about the HIV virus and other STD's. She shared horror stories with them that caused them to not want to even look at a man for a while. Of course this situation proves that the effect of it only lasted a short time. Emerald went to see her that very same day.

"Hey sis," she said as she entered Pamela's office. "Um, hum," Pamela said in a what do you want, I know you're up to something voice. "What's the um, hum all about," Emerald asked in an innocent tone? "Chile, I know you better than you know yourself. What have you done?" "I, I need a pregnancy test," Emerald stuttered and tightly closed her eyes to prepare for Pamela to yell at her. "You need a what? Girl did you use all those condoms I gave you and Flora? What is wrong with you? I talk to you all the time. If you are pregnant I'm going to kill you and bring you back to life so I don't go to jail. Come on in the bathroom." Emerald tolerated Pamela talking to her in that tone because she was older by ten years, married and had three children of her own. She was also an Evangelist and Emerald respected her. She was the big sister that Emerald didn't have. She always told her and Flora to not have sex but begged them to at least protect themselves if they did. So she was very angry at Emerald right now.

"I'm not trying to be graphic Emerald but there's something that I have to know. Why didn't you protect yourself? What happened? Did the condom break?" "No Pamela, the condom didn't break," Emerald said with her head held down while Pamela prepared the pregnancy test for her. "So then, what happened," Pamela asked Emerald with her hands on her hips? "We didn't use a condom the last time we slept together," Emerald said quietly. "We used the withdraw method. I got pregnant from pre-ejaculation." Emerald looked into Pamela's eyes for the first time that day and saw that Pamela was more hurt than angry. "Here's the test Emerald. Urinate in the cup and knock on the window when you're done." With that, she left.

Emerald was so scared that she couldn't even urinate to take the test. She knew the results that she took at home were right. Never the less, there was something about getting this final confirmation that snapped Emerald back. It brought her to the realization of what was happening in her life. Emerald left the restroom and told Pamela that she was too nervous and couldn't use the test. Pamela let her take it home and promised to come over after six o' clock to help her.

The entire day was torture for Emerald. She talked to her mom on a daily basis but couldn't call her today because she knew that she would cry on the telephone. She did everything that she could to keep busy and attempt to remove her thoughts from her situation. But nothing worked.

Would six o' clock ever get there? "Pamela please hurry. I'm dying," thought Emerald. Finally Pamela arrived. She rang the doorbell three times and Emerald about fell out from worry when she opened the door for Pamela to come in. "Girl you are in trouble," she cooed and laughed. "Just give me the test," whined Emerald. "There you go," Pamela said.

Emerald took the test and it was confirmed. She was going to be a mother, and a single mother at that. Now she had to decide how, when and where she would tell her parents about the one thing that would hurt them. Their unmarried daughter that they raised so well was eight weeks pregnant and scheduled to preach her first sermon in two weeks.

CHAPTER 5

Saturday morning arrived and she was off from work thank God. She opened her eyes and peeked out of the window to see what type of day it was. It was a cold, wet and cloudy day. It was a day where you just cuddled in bed with a remote and Chinese food or pizza all day. It was a lazy day. The wind rustled against her bedroom window and she pulled the covers closer to her chin. After the week that Emerald had, she could stand to be lazy and just rest. She rubbed her stomach and thought of her unborn child. "In a few months, I won't be able to stay in bed all day or night for that matter," she thought. She would be up tending to her child. The ringing of the telephone interrupted her thoughts. It was her younger sister Janelle. Janelle needed her hair permed so of course she called Emerald. Emerald was doing hair since her teenage years. Her hands were blessed to grow hair and she enjoyed doing it. She wanted to go to hair school but her parents suggested that she obtain a degree in something else first. Well because her heart was into hair and not into business, which was her major, she wasn't focused.

Emerald never had a problem doing anything for Janelle. She was of course Emerald's only sister. The problem was though that Janelle didn't drive so their mother, Louise would have to bring her to Emerald's house. However, Emerald agreed to do her sister's hair anyway. She got out of bed to take a shower and prepare for the upcoming event. She'd have to tell her mother. They were so close. It was impossible for Emerald to keep anything away from her. As she thought of telling her mother, the tears ran down her caramel colored face. "I have to tell her. I'm going to tell her," she thought. As she showered, she prayed to God and asked him to forgive her for sleeping with Tony in the first place.

She told him that she needed his strength. She felt so alone and he was the only one that would be able to keep her sane right now. "I need you Lord," is what she said repeatedly. Soon she felt calm enough to stand up and do what needed to be done. She was going to look her mom in the face and tell her the truth.

She dressed herself and went into the kitchen to prepare a slice of toast. She wasn't hungry but still needed to feed the little one inside of her. She ate slowly, deliberately savoring every flavor of the buttered piece of bread. She drank a cup of hot tea with a hint of mint.

Why did I have to be so anxious to have a man in my life? If I had just been comfortable in the state that I was in, a single, black female, working on a promising job and enjoying life then I wouldn't be in this mess right now! That is however, what age, jealousy, and the influence of others will do to you if you allow it. I am twenty-four years old. My mother was married by now when she was my age. Some of the church members nagged me constantly about not having a husband or not even dating anyone. I allowed it to get to me. My best friend is married with a little girl. I am still single. I use to think that I was ugly or too skinny. I

used to think that there must be something
about me that caused me to still be single at
twenty-four. Why could I not stay in a
relationship? Why was I not good enough to
be loved?

The chiming of the doorbell ended her
thoughts. It was Louise and Janelle. Her
stomach sank. Her mouth went dry. She
wanted to wake from this nightmare and
start over. This is all a dream. It wasn't a
dream though. It was very real. As real as
her mother standing in the doorway and the
fetus in her womb.

CHAPTER 6

"Hey boo," Louise said as she kissed her
daughter on the forehead and walked into
the warm apartment. "Hey mom," sighed
Emerald. She was praying that her mother
wouldn't notice that her eyes were swollen
from crying. She tried to avoid looking her
in the eyes because of it. "What you got to
eat? I'm hungry," Janelle chimed in.
"Nothing, I haven't cooked yet." Emerald
sat down at the kitchen table because she
was feeling lightheaded. Janelle hung her
coat in the hall closet and grabbed the
remote to turn on the television. Emerald
took a deep breath and quickly said, "Mom I
have something to tell you." All of a sudden
it seemed like someone had dumped a
bucket of water on her face. Her tears began

to flow endlessly. Her mother rushed over to her and sat down. "Emerald what's wrong with you? Why are you crying? What happened," her mother asked? Emerald wiped her face with her sleeves and Janelle brought her a Kleenex. Janelle stood by her chair with a concerned look on her face and rubbed her sisters back. It broke her heart to see her sister crying. All the while she was praying that it was something that she could possibly help her with. Emerald continued to sob harder and harder. "What's wrong Emerald? You're beginning to scare me," Louise said. Janelle was in shock because in all of her nineteen years she had never seen her sister breakdown like this.

"Mom, I'm so sorry," Emerald cried. "Sorry for what? What's going on? Janelle call your daddy. Get him over here right now!" "No, no please don't call daddy. I'm ok. I promise," Emerald threw in. She quickly dried her eyes. "Ok well if you're ok then why are you crying," Louise asked? "I'm pregnant Mom," Emerald hurriedly said. "You're what," Louise said while rising from the table? Janelle felt like her legs were going to give in so she took a seat at the table next to Emerald. "I'm pregnant." "No, uh-uh, no you're lying. I know better," Louise said with tears filling her eyes. "Mom, I'm sorry," Emerald said. Emerald's heart broke in two watching the tears form in her mother's eyes. "I don't believe it. Have you been to the doctor? Who told you that you were pregnant? Have you had symptoms," Louise asked all at once without giving Emerald a chance to answer one at a time? Emerald sniffed and dabbed the corners of her eyes. "I took an EPT test two days ago and I went to the Doctor yesterday and got a professional test. I will meet with my OB-GYN on Tuesday."

Emerald continued to sob. Janelle sat still in the corner of the table and cried. When Emerald looked into her mother's eyes, she saw hurt, disappointment, anger and the need to kill Tony but deep inside her mother's eyes, Emerald saw love.

Louise pulled Emerald to her feet and hugged her. "Don't cry Emerald. You don't need to be upset right now. You need to be stress free so the baby can be healthy," Louise said. "It's going to be alright," she said as she held Emerald away from her by the shoulders. "You hear me Emerald? It's going to be alright," Louise reassured Emerald.

Emerald saw the buildings in her world that had previously crash begin to get up off of the ground. She saw the leaves on the trees turn green again in her mind. Her mother still loved her and that was all she needed to hear right now.

Her mother walked away from her. "What is Tony saying about all this? Your sermon is in two weeks. Are you still going to go through with it? You're going to have to tell your Daddy this one. I can't do it," Louise said all in one breath it seemed. "Tony and I broke up Mom. He said he needed a break so I made it permanent for him," Emerald said. "He did what," Louise yelled? "After all we've done for his sorry behind?" "It's ok Mom. I will survive without him," Emerald consoled her. "Yes you will as long as your Daddy and I are here," she said.

"What about your sermon," she asked again? This time giving Emerald the chance to answer her. "I don't know what's going to happen with that. I have to talk to Pastor Dudley." "Ok, ok, it will be alright," Louise said in a soothing voice that calmed Emerald even the more. No matter how old Emerald got, her parent's feelings and input were always important to her. She needed their support even if not financially but just emotionally. She was glad to know that she had it!

Emerald hugged her mom tightly and thanked her. Louise kissed Emerald's forehead again. She grabbed Emerald's chin. "Everyone makes mistakes Emerald but you pick yourself up and move on. I was young when I got pregnant with you. Look at you now. You're all grown up, on your own, got your own car, a good job and your smart Emerald. You have the power to do and be anything that you want. Life is not over, it's only begun. This is a disappointing situation but you're not a disappointment to me Emerald. I'm proud of you baby, you've done well for yourself." Louise smiled at her daughter. Emerald just grinned like a five-year-old little girl.

"Now let's figure out how we're going to tell your father. In the meantime please do something with Janelle's hair. She looks like something from the lost and found." They both looked at Janelle's hair and fell over laughing. She definitely needed something 'done' to it! Janelle rolled her eyes at them and laughed too.

Emerald relaxed Janelle's hair, gave her a deep conditioning treatment and roller set it. It turned out beautiful. It was shiny and full of body when Emerald was through. Emerald smiled at her product and wished she had her Cosmetology license. "One day," she thought, "I'll get it."

CHAPTER 7

Later that night Emerald called her father, Marcus. "Hey Daddy," she said, sounding like a teenager that wrecked the car. "Hey Emerald. What's going on," Marcus asked? "Not much," Emerald replied. "Daddy, you know I love you right?" "Yep," he said. "Well, daddy, I have to tell you something. I'm just going to come out and say it and get it over with. I've had enough moments today to last me a lifetime." "Ok what is it," Marcus asked? "Daddy I'm pregnant. Tony and I broke up and I'm ok with that," Emerald said. "I don't want you to worry about me. I'm ok, really. And yes, I've already told mom."

His only reply was Ok as he took several deep breathes. He said ok about four more times. He then said, "Ok said Emerald, it will be alright. I'll see you at church tomorrow. I love you Emerald," Marcus said. "I love you too Daddy." "Goodnight Emerald." They hung up the phone.

Emerald could hardly speak because she was crying so hard. She dried her eyes and poured herself a glass of ginger ale. Well, I might as well call Pastor Dudley. She dialed his number and waited for someone to answer. "Hello," he sang into the receiver. He was always so cheerful. "Hey Pastor how are you?" "Is this Emerald?" "Yes sir this is Emerald." "How are ya," he asked? "Not so good Pastor," Emerald slowly said. "What's wrong," he asked with so much concern in his voice? "Will you not be able to do praise and worship tomorrow?" "I don't know Pastor." "Are you sick?" "No Pastor but I do have something to tell you." "Ok," he said, "what is it?" "Pastor Dudley I just found out that I'm pregnant. I know my sermon is in two weeks. So I was wondering if you would want to cancel it?"

"Well, that depends Emerald. Did you repent," he asked? "Huh," asked Emerald sounding confused? "Did you repent," Pastor Dudley repeated? "Yes sir." "Then we will keep our date. Emerald I want you to understand something. The baby is not the sin! That baby is a gift from God. When you laid down with that man the sin was committed. I love you Emerald and God loves you too. He just hates the sin that you committed. But he is a forgiving God so if we have him in our hearts then we should be forgiving too. God knew this day would come long before you were even born. Now dust yourself off and move on. Go and sin no more. Now let me ask you again, are you doing praise and worship tomorrow?"

"Yes sir." "That's my girl, see you in the morning Emerald." "Ok Pastor Dudley." Emerald slept well that night.

CHAPTER 8

Church was a press for Emerald. Talking to her father on the phone was one thing but seeing the hurt in his eyes would be something else. She could hardly dress herself from running to the bathroom to vomit. If she made it to the bathroom before messing up herself and the floor. It was funny how she'd just found out that she was pregnant but morning sickness seemed to have fallen out of the sky upon her. Morning sickness went into noonday sickness and noonday into evening and evening into nighttime sickness. No hour of the day went undone from her feeling ill. She decided to wear black today. Because although there was something living on the inside of her she still felt like she was dying.

The yard of Mt. New James We Fight for Our Own, Back in the Woods Church was packed. She felt like today's service would be featuring her. Everyone that greeted her seemed to have already heard the news. Soon to be Evangelist Emerald Sinclair was pregnant. She went toward the Pastor's study and knocked on the door. Immediately he said, "Come in." She eased her way into the study and said, "Good morning Pastor." "Good morning Sis. Emerald," he said while giving her a hug. "How are you feeling?" "A little nauseated, nervous and scared out of my mind but other than that I'm alright." "Oh Emerald you're a survivor. This will not take you down," he said with determination. "You are anointed and called by God. You just made a mistake as we all have. Remember that there is no big sin or little sin. Sin is just sin. What makes you different from a lot of the people out in the audience is that you've repented and they haven't."

Emerald unconvincingly smiled and told him that she was going to go and prepare for praise and worship. As she walked away the knots in her stomach got tighter and tighter. I can do this she told herself. I am a survivor. She walked onto the podium and began praise and worship. The people sung, danced and cried as they all praised the Lord with her. Emerald normally closed her eyes as she sung but this particular day she looked around at all of the people participating with her and wondered how they would treat her once they found out that she was carrying a child in her belly and she was still single. At the mere thought of it she felt tears swelling in her eyes. She tried to hold back but she caught her father's eye as he walked in and it was all over! She sung the words, "I love you, I love you, I love you Lord today, because you cared for me in such a special way, etc...." The audience sung with her while worshipping

God. When she looked up again both of her parents were standing with their hands raised and tears flowing as if they were at a funeral. Emerald lost it. She turned to the Pastor and ended praise and worship. She went to the bathroom and boiled over. Pamela and Flora whom were also members of her church came rushing in behind her. They didn't say anything; they just held her as she wept. She heard one of them sniff and said "it's going to be alright." But it didn't sound like Pamela or Flora. She looked up and Pamela and Flora were crying but they had stepped back. Her mother and father were standing over her. Her mother's voice was the one that she heard as her father handed her his handkerchief with an M for Marcus embroidded on it. He whispered in her ear, "You are going to make a fantastic mother Emerald, a fantastic mother." She fell into his arms, this time crying tears of joy.

CHAPTER 9

After church Emerald went over to her parent's house for dinner. The smell of soul food filled the air. Louise made collard greens, honey baked ham with pineapples, macaroni and cheese and fried chicken. She'd also purchased a Sara Lee French Strawberry Cheesecake, which was Emerald's favorite dessert. Emerald had some of everything and seconds of it too.

She even took a plate to go. No one spoke of her pregnancy in a negative way. They simply teased her about how big she was getting and how her appetite was already increasing incredibly.

The evening ended with hugs and kisses as usual as Emerald left and prepared to take the thirty-minute drive to her apartment on the other side of town. As she drove, she rubbed her stomach and smiled. I love you whoever you are. I am going to give you all the love that a mother can give a child even if I have to do it all by myself. She leaned her head on the headrest, turned up her radio and continued the drive home.

When she pulled into her driveway, Tony was parked near her door. He must have been there for a while because when she got out of her vehicle and looked into his, he was asleep. She knocked on his window and startled him. He looked around as if he didn't know where he was at first and then reality slapped him in the face. Emerald chuckled at the thought of her slapping him into reality. She waited on him to get out of his truck. When he stepped out Emerald's mind seemed to spin. He looked delightfully delicious in some black slacks, black shoes and a red muscle shirt that clung just right! Covering his entire body was a black leather coat. God was going to have to keep her tonight!

It was thirty-five degrees outside but Emerald's body seemed like it was a blazing fire. He came up to her and pecked her on the lips suddenly. It excited Emerald but she backed up and said, "Don't do that Tony!" "What's wrong with you," Tony asked as he waited on Emerald to unlock the door to her home? "Nothing's wrong with me but everything is wrong with you," she said as they walked into the house. She stepped into the kitchen to put her food up and he followed her. "Baby what's that suppose to mean." "First of all, Emerald said pointing her finger at his face, I'm not your baby. I'm carrying your baby. Second of all, do you have Alzheimer's or something? I told you we were through. You have a permanent break from me remember? Now I'm tired. It's been a long day and I'm not in the mood for foolishness tonight."

She felt his arms encircling her widening waist. "Come on baby don't be like that," Tony replied pleadingly. She felt his body calling out to her. She tried to move his hands off of her but she was not physically strong enough. He had a grip on her. "I miss you," he said. Before she knew it he spun her around to face him and kissed her so tenderly she thought she was floating. It took everything in her to gain the will to resist him. Relentlessly, she pulled away. "Tony, I said stop." She looked more determined than she felt. On the inside she was doing a cartwheel for the mere fact that she was standing up to him. She'd never denied him before so he was in shock. However, deep down inside, she almost felt like it was turning him on. Never the less, she had to stay focused. "What's wrong, you don't miss me Emerald? You don't love me anymore," Tony asked with a sadden look on his face as he allowed her to step back from his grasp?

"Here's the deal Tony, I have a lot on my plate and dealing with you is not what I have a taste for right now." "Yeah, well what exactly do you have a taste for," he asked while walking towards her again? Emerald had to think just to respond because her body wanted to leap into his arms and beckon him to take her right there. She backed into the pantry door and had nowhere to go. "I want you so bad right now Emerald. You look so sexy being pregnant." He hovered over her with his tall frame and she felt like she was going to suffocate. Her flesh and her spirit were in a literal fight. It was up to her which one would win. "Well we could have been married and this wouldn't have been a problem but you didn't want me or this baby remember?"

"Ah man, here you go," Tony said. "Look Tony, the only things that you and I need to discuss are my doctor appointments and your attendance." "No problem when is the first one, Tony asked." "This Tuesday at 9 am. Here's the address. You can meet me there," Emerald said. "Yeah alright," Tony nonchalantly said.

Emerald walked to the door. Ok goodnight Tony. "Are you serious, is that really it," he asked? Emerald nodded her head yes. "So we can't even watch a movie or something?" "No, we can't! Goodnight Tony," Emerald persisted. She opened the door and waited for him to leave. "Alright then, fine," he said and pouted his way out of her home.

She closed the door behind her and held her stomach. It wasn't until she felt the coolness drop on her neck that she realized that she had been crying.

CHAPTER 10
Sleep was the only resolve for her. Her body was in physical need of companionship but her spirit was in need of a closer relationship with God. She was proud of how she'd handled herself tonight. The rush

that she got from doing the right thing was
so much better than a five-minute thrill of
sin. But for now she needed some relief and
to get her mind off of him and what just
happened. Emerald decided to take a long
hot shower and go to bed. While showering
she prayed for continuous strength to stay in
the will of God.

Sleep didn't come easy for her. She tossed
and turned for most of the night. When she
did fall asleep, she dreamt of lounging in a
room of all white furniture and decorations.
She looked to be about seven or eight
months pregnant. She was dressed in a thin,
spaghetti strapped, white silk dress that
clung to her every curve. She also had a
white flower in her hair. She laid on the
couch while Tony, dressed in white knelt
beside her. He kissed her belly while telling
her how beautiful she looked. They
laughed, hugged, and kissed throughout the
dream but when he pulled away Tony was
not himself. The man in the dream was her
long time friend, Rayne.

Emerald awoke abruptly to the sound of the
alarm clock going off. It was only a dream
she thought. And a dream about Rayne.
Now that's funny. Rayne was a friend of
Emerald for the past four years. He was
interested in her but the feelings were far
from mutual.

Emerald rubbed her eyes and got out of bed. All of a sudden she had to hold on to the bed pole as the room seemed to twirl around her. She held one hand over her mouth and dashed towards the toilet. Every time she tried to get up and get herself together for work she ended up with her face in the toilet again.

She could hardly walk. She crawled to the nightstand in her room and reached up for the phone. She dialed her job and called into work. She had plenty of personal time and sick leave that could be used so she was certainly grateful for that. She managed to stand and slowly walk into the kitchen where Flora was. She told her how badly she was feeling because of the pregnancy. Flora made her some hot tea and toast to settle her stomach. She promised to make dinner that evening and left for work. Emerald got a pillow and blanket and laid on the sofa in the living room. She turned on the television and flipped through the remote trying to find something interesting to watch. Nothing moved her so she allowed it to stay on one of the children's channels. She looked around the apartment and thought of all the good times she'd had there. Days and nights filled with laughter. Some tears were shed also but she weathered every storm. She wondered how she was going to weather this storm though. Tony wanted to be a player and she didn't have time for that. She had a whole new life and a baby to plan for. As for now, it looked like it would be without Tony.

While in deep thought, she heard the mailman and went to see what had come for her. Most of the mail she threw on the table. However, she came across an envelope that looked quite interesting. It was from her landlord. The letter stated that they're rent was going up another fifty dollars. The rent was already borderline too expensive. She looked around the room again. Where would the playpen go, the stroller, the swing, the toys, the baby's clothes, etc.? How would Flora handle having a baby here with us? How would she handle the baby waking every two hours for feeding? She would find out as soon as Flora came home. As for now however, Emerald decided to go back to bed, order something terribly, unhealthy to eat and relax for the remainder of the day. She ordered and ate pizza. The sleep came easily.

CHAPTER 11

It was seven in the evening when Emerald woke to the smell of fried chicken and something sweet. She hadn't planned on sleeping in that long but your body always tells you what you need and after a while it insists on getting it. She slowly sat up in the bed and looked around at the cold pizza sitting on her nightstand. There was an empty bottle of soda beside it. The remote control was on the floor near her house shoes. It must have fallen off of the bed while she was asleep. She got up and went into the shower. While there she remembered all of the times that she'd spent in that very same spot, except with Tony accompanying her there. She quickly got rid of those thoughts and did what she needed to do and got out of the shower. She clothed herself in a pair of black sweatpants, an oversized t-shirt and went into the living room. Flora was dancing to Whitney Houston's, *"I'm Every Woman, it's All in Me."* Emerald just sat on the couch and laughed.

She envied the thought that Flora had not a care in the world. She, on the other hand, had one hundred and one things to think about. "How was your day," Flora asked while still dancing? "It was ok," Emerald replied. "I guess it was since you slept all day," Flora said. "Girl I was tired. Hey by the way did you see the letter from our landlord on the table? I left it there for you." "Yeah I saw it alright. I was thinking about moving back home with my mother anyway. I need to save some money." That slapped Emerald in the face. It shouldn't

have though. It wasn't like she and Flora
had signed a contract to be together until
they death do them part!

"What are your plans," Flora asked
Emerald? "Huh, oh, I don't know. What I
do know is that I won't be able to afford that
high rent expense. Especially by myself if
you're moving out. I guess I need to start
looking for a cheaper place. But you know
me; I'm not about to live in a ghetto place.
I'll pay for my safety. But I'm going to
need a lot of space too with a baby around."

"Yeah, speaking of, have you talked to
Pastor Dudley yet," Flora asked? "Yep I
talked to him." "Well, what did he say,"
Flora asked anxiously? "We're still going to
go forth with everything." "Wow. Was he
disappointed," Flora questioned more? "I'm
sure he was but he didn't display it to me.
He just encouraged me." "Man, that's rare,"
Flora said in a daze. "Yes, it is definitely
rare," Emerald responded. "Thank God for a
real leader."

"In the meantime though, I'm struggling."
"Struggling with what," Flora asked while
nibbling on a chocolate chip cookie? "Girl,
you don't miss something that you've never
had. Once you've had it—you miss it. I'm
just trying to stay focused on God but it's
hard when you're use to having someone

there and they just up and leave you."
"Yeah I know but you'll make it Emerald."

"I know I will but it's still hard. People think that just because you're saved, that you don't go through anything. When you're saved, you go through more! Everyday there's a struggle just to stay saved. I love the Lord but it's a battle between your flesh and your spirit. One must yield to the other. My struggle right now is making sure that I allow the Holy Spirit to rule and my flesh to submit."

"Girl you're not telling me anything that I don't know. Been there, done that and sometimes I think I'm still there," Flora said.

"Tony came by the other night Flora and I think the only thing that kept me from sleeping with him is where I'm going in God and the fact that I can't afford to mess up or be hurt again. I mean it's like the enemy himself sent him here. I wish the church had a support group for singles or something. The married people have tapes, books, and etc. They can set up meetings and talk to the Pastor about there problems. I can't tell my Pastor, who's married, whose wife is not a preacher that my flesh is acting up. That's how so many Pastors get caught up in adultery today. I think that it is just inappropriate to talk to your Pastor about that. He's human too."

Flora jumped in, " Could you imagine if we could have single people meetings and be able to talk freely about what we go through?" "Exactly," Emerald said in agreement. "It's like married people forget what they went through when they were single. Like they just spoke in tongues all day and their flesh never craved anything that it shouldn't have," Flora continued.

"There was some preacher on television that said something important when she talked about married people not being able to tell her anything about being single. I think her name is Prophetess Juanita Bynum. But she talked about people being married for a long time forgetting what it was like being single but they try to tell you to hold out. Chile' please."

"Emerald I think we need to go and find that preacher and have lunch or something because she seems to be the only who's understanding the singles right now besides Bishop T.D. Jakes. I'm sure there are more people out there but we just don't know about them," Flora said. "Well I hope they appear soon because we need help," Emerald said while laughing. The scent of the food that Flora cooked seemed to sweep pass Emerald's nostrils.

PART 2

RAYNE ON ME!!!!!

CHAPTER 12

"Um, that food smells righteous. Is it ready yet," Emerald asked while rubbing her belly? "Yeah, I'm going to go ahead and eat as well so that I can go to bed. It's been a long day," Flora said as she yawned and walked into the kitchen.

Emerald and Flora ate, talked some more and Flora went to bed. Emerald went into her bedroom to prepare herself for her Doctor's appointment the next day. "Tony probably won't even show up," she thought. Just then, the telephone rang. "Phone Emerald," Flora yelled to her. "Who is it," Emerald asked sounding annoyed because she didn't feel like talking? "Your real husband, Mr. Rayne Washington," Flora said laughingly. "I got it," Emerald said while rolling her eyes.

Rayne Washington was a long time friend of Emerald's. She'd met him four years ago. The first day that she met him he told her that the Lord said that she was going to be his wife. She didn't hear the Lord say that nor did she want to hear it. Rayne was fine. He stood right at 6'0" and carried 200lbs of straight hard muscle. Working out was a ritual for him. He had dark cocoa skin and wore two hooped earrings in both ears. He also wore green contacts. He was definitely eye candy but he was too sweet for her. He gave her anything that she asked for. But she needed or wanted a man that told her no every once and a while!

So for the past four years, his sending flowers, buying gifts, spending time with her was all worthless as far as she was concerned but her family and friends thought differently. Flora and Louise, Emerald's mother, were Rayne's biggest cheerleaders.

She put the phone to her ears and said, "Hello." "Hey Lady how are you," the deep, silky voice of Rayne asked? His voice alone would send most women into a frenzy but it didn't affect Emerald at all!

"I'm good and you," she answered. "I'm fine. Headed home tomorrow. I was wondering if I could come and see you," Rayne said with hope in his voice.

"No, I'll be busy tomorrow but maybe another day." "Ok," Rayne sadly said but tried to still remain pleasant.

"Hey you do know that my initial sermon is in two weeks right? Do you think you'll be able to sing for me," Emerald asked? "Of course I'll sing for you. You know I've got your back," Rayne replied sounding borderline too excited. "Ok well I'll see you then," Emerald said trying to end the call.

"Wait a minute, how has your boyfriend treating you," Rayne asked sounding mischievous? "Uh, I don't want to talk about him right now," Emerald quickly said. "Why, what's wrong? Do you need me to come down there," Rayne questioned?

"No, no, I'm fine. There's just something going on that's all." "Well you know if you need anything, I'm here for you," Rayne said in a comforting way that warmed Emerald inside. "Yes, I know. Well listen, I really have to go so I'll talk to you later," Emerald said rushing him off of the phone. "Ok Lady, be encouraged." "I will and thanks, bye bye."

Rayne worked away from home as a truck driver. But if Emerald ever needed him, he'd be there. She looked forward to him singing at her initial sermon. He was so anointed. Everyone loved hearing him sing. She wondered how he'd react when he found out that she was pregnant. I better tell him before he makes the trip. I'll call him tomorrow she decided. He'll be in town so I'll ask him to come over after all.

CHAPTER 13

Emerald rose the following morning and prepared herself to leave for her Doctor's appointment. When she arrived she signed in and sat in the waiting area. The mere smell of the doctor's office made her nauseous. The main door opened and in came in Tony. He was late as usual. He sat next to her and asked how she was. "I'm fine," she replied while looking straight ahead. "Are you nervous," he asked? "Very." They laughed. "You think it's a girl or a boy?" "I don't know," she said. "As sick as I've been I think it's a girl. A lot of people say that girls take you through."

"Emerald Sinclair," the nurse called. "You want me to come back there with you," Tony asked? "It doesn't matter," Emerald responded nonchalantly. Emerald and Tony entered the backroom where they weighed her, stuck her, poked her, questioned her and some of everything else. They also did an ultrasound. There it was, a real baby, living and growing on the inside of her. Tony sat there smiling. Emerald wondered what he was thinking.

When the appointment was over Tony walked her to her car. "I'm starved, you want to go grab something to eat," Tony asked? "From where," she inquired? "How about some seafood," he implied? "That's fine." "You can ride with me and I'll bring you back to your car," Tony offered.

They rode in silence for a while. "I really do miss you Emerald." She continued to look straight ahead. "I'm just not ready for this," he continued. Emerald remained silent. "Pull the car over," she said abruptly. "Emerald come on don't act like that," Tony pleaded. "Pull the car over or have vomit all up and through here," she demanded.

He pulled over so fast that he almost hit the car next to them. She jumped out and regurgitated. He never got out. He just handed her some napkins while he frowned at her. She wiped her mouth and got back in the truck. She dug in her purse for a peppermint to hopefully settle her stomach. She found one and leaned her head against the headrest.

"Thanks for caring so much," she said sarcastically. "What do you mean?" "You could've rubbed my back or something not just sit there and look disgusted." "Whatever," Tony's replied. Emerald rolled her eyes and wished she'd never agreed to lunch with him.

They arrived at the restaurant and Tony made small talk the entire time. He occasionally flirted with Emerald and she occasionally cut him short. Their lunch ended and he drove her back to her car. Before she got out of his truck he said to her, "the doctor said your only nine weeks along in this pregnancy. It's not too late you know." "It's not too late for what Tony?" Emerald knew what he meant but couldn't believe that he was saying it. "It's not too late for you to get rid of it. I'll give you the money. I was kind of hoping that we could go and have it done today," Tony said.

"So that was your motive for coming with me to the Doctor and asking me out to lunch." "You know what Tony, you are even more of a donkey then I thought you were." With that said and Tony's mouth stuck open, Emerald got out of his truck, into her car and sped off. She was so angry that she was fussing and no one was there. Her cell phone rang. "HELLO," she yelled. "Hey, are you ok," the person asked? "Yes, but who is this," Emerald snapped? "This is Rayne. Are you sure you're ok?" "Hey Rayne, I'm sorry." "What's wrong baby?" "I just had an argument with Tony that's all." "He didn't hit you did he," Rayne asked anxiously? "No, he's stupid not crazy," Emerald replied. "True," Rayne said. "Listen, Rayne, I really have to talk to you, can you come over? I'll be home in about ten minutes." "Sure," Rayne said worriedly, "I'm on my way."

As usual when Rayne arrived, he arrived
with flowers as he did now. How he got to
pick up flowers and be at Emerald's house
within ten minutes, no one will ever know
but him. The flowers were white roses in a
beautiful lavender vase with the poem
"footprints" written on it. She told him how
beautiful they were. She hugged and
thanked him. When Emerald hugged Rayne
this time however, she felt something
different. Something tugged at her heart.
She felt something this time that she'd never
felt before.

"Are you sure you're ok," Rayne questioned
Emerald? "Yes I'm alright. I'm just sick of
him that's all." "What happened, if you
don't mind me asking?" "No, it's no
problem," Emerald said with a wave of her
hand. "I trust you. Have a seat Rayne."
Emerald sat next to him and held one of his
hands that was placed on his knee. Fire shot
through Rayne and he had to remember to
contain himself.

"Rayne, I have something very important to
tell you that may cause you to be upset.
Honestly speaking, I don't know if you'll
want to be my friend anymore." "Emerald,
you're making me nervous. What's wrong,"
Rayne asked sitting on the edge of his seat?
"Rayne, I know how you feel about me and I
don't want to hurt you. But before you

came down next week I needed to be honest with you." "Ok, what is it," Rayne asked becoming annoyed at her procrastination? "Just say it! I can handle it, I promise." "Ok, here goes." Emerald kept her gaze on his hand instead of his eyes. She couldn't bare to see the hurt in them that she knew would come. "Rayne, I'm pregnant with Tony's baby." Emerald sputtered it out of her mouth faster than she knew she could talk. "You're what?" Rayne snatched the hand that Emerald was holding away? He reacted like he'd been momentarily struck by electricity. "I'm pregnant with," Emerald attempted to repeat. "I heard you," Rayne cut her off.

"I didn't know if you would still want to sing at my initial sermon or not." "Man," Rayne sighed. Emerald looked at Rayne's face, for the first time and saw that tears ran from his eyes. "Oh my God Rayne, you're crying," Emerald said in shock. "I'm so sorry. I never meant to hurt you," Emerald proclaimed apologetically. "I'm crying because reality has just sunk in," Rayne said looking forward instead of at Emerald. " I'm actually realizing that I really don't have a chance with you." He rubbed his forehead and moaned. "So, have you guys moved the wedding date up?" He glanced her way and then quickly turned from her. "No, we haven't." "And you're still going to go

through with the first sermon?" "Yes."
"Ok, well I guess I'll see you at your first
sermon." "Are you serious," Emerald asked
almost leaping off of the sofa? "Yeah man.
I just hope that Tony treats you right."
Emerald lowered her head and looked away.
She didn't have the courage to tell Rayne
that she and Tony were not together
anymore. If he knew that he would've
dropped on his knees and asked her to marry
him right then. And deep down inside,
Emerald was feeling like she'd say yes.

CHAPTER 14
When Rayne left Emerald's house she
decided to work on her sermon. She thought
about all that happened the past few days
and especially the conversation that she'd
had with Flora. Immediately, her sermon's
topic came to her. She decided to use 'You
can have life in the spirit if you kill the
flesh, as her topic'. She came from Romans
8:1 of the King James Bible, "There is
therefore now no condemnation to them that
walk not after the flesh but after the spirit."

Once she prepared her message she
proofread it. She was definitely preaching
to herself. Her flesh had to die. She had to
daily take on the mind of Christ in order to
have power over her fleshly desires. In this
new place in God also come new devils.
She had to be strong enough to resist

temptation. She prepared her message and prepared herself mentally and spiritually.

Before she knew it, the big day had arrived. At eight that morning, Rayne called. "Hello." "Hey Lady how are you?" Emerald blushed. "Hey Rayne I'm fine." She couldn't understand why she was feeling all goo-goo-gah-gah over him all of a sudden. "You ready for tonight," Rayne asked? "As ready as I'll ever be." "Well I was confirming that you still want me to sing. I'm driving from California as we speak," Rayne said. "California, what in the world," Emerald said feeling flattered? "Where are you now?"

"I'm in North Carolina and it's snowing like crazy. I've been driving for the past three days trying to get there. No disrespect Emerald, I know that you have a man and all but I love you with all my heart. I know you don't love me but, Rayne hesitated, I just need to be there that's all." (What Rayne wasn't and couldn't tell Emerald was that when he was in California the Lord spoke to him and told him to go and get his wife. Today would be the day of transition in there friendship.) "Ok," was all Emerald could say. "So I guess I'll meet the lucky man tonight," Rayne insinuated. "I guess," Emerald said in a low tone. "Ok then I'll see you tonight." "Ok Rayne, Bye."

Emerald thought to herself, "Oh my God, what am I going to do? It's my big day. Even though Tony and I aren't on good terms I thought he would have at least called by now." Just then, the doorbell rang. Emerald threw her bathrobe on and went to answer the door. She peeped through the peephole and saw that it was someone with flowers. She opened the door. "May I help you?" "Are you Emerald," the gentleman asked with flowers practically covering his face? "Yes, I am." "This is from Rayne," he said while handing her the bouquet of flowers. The gentleman looked just like Rayne. He smiled as he looked into her face. "I've heard a lot about you. You must be special because Rayne don't buy flowers for no female except our mom," he said in an exaggerated tone! "Our Mom," Emerald thought to herself? "You're Rayne's brother?" "Yeah, that's me," he said while smiling proudly and walking away. "Hey by the way, congrats on your sermon. You take care of yourself," he yelled. "You too," she yelled out to him.

She smiled and closed the door. He said that Rayne never bought flowers for females. She got them all the time. She looked into the flowers and pulled out the card. It read, "When you're anointed, you're just anointed! Your Friend, Rayne." She called

him back. When he answered he didn't say
hello but instead, he answered with, "Did
you like your morning arrival?" "I did.
Thank you so much," Emerald said feeling
like a five-year old on Christmas morning.
"Your welcome," he said, feeling thrilled
that he'd made her smile. "You know you
didn't have to do that." "Yes, but I wanted
to." "Thank you Rayne, you're so sweet."
"Yeah I know." They both laughed.
"Alright well I guess we'll see each other in
a few hours," Emerald said ending the call.
"Ok, Bye," he said.

Emerald didn't realize how hard she was
smiling until she bumped into Flora leaning
on the kitchen counter with a sheepish grin
on her face. "Um, flowers. Not from Tony
I'm sure. Rayne more than likely and
you're grinning from ear to ear!"
"Whatever," Emerald said and went back to
her room-still smiling. Flora came rushing
in like a mother about to spank a child. "I
don't know why you won't give that boy a
chance! He's so in love with you that he
doesn't know if he's coming or going."
"Yeah, yeah, yeah," Emerald said brushing
off Flora's comments. "I just don't like him
like that." "All right Emerald, but don't
pass up your blessings," Flora said sounding
like an old grandma for real. "Flora get out
of my room," she said while laughing. Flora

walked out shaking her head and laughing too.

CHAPTER 15

It was four p.m. and in one hour Emerald would be at the church for her sermon. Butterflies swam in her stomach. She dressed and vomited at the same time. Lord please help me, she inwardly prayed. She grabbed a bath towel, saltine crackers, ginger ale and a trash bag just in case she had an encounter on the road. Flora left already. She got in her car and headed for church. When she arrived the churchyard was filled with cars. Cars were even parked on the side of the road. Emerald became so scared that she thought she'd pass out.

Out of all of the vehicles that were there, the one vehicle that she didn't see was Tony's. That saddened her a bit but she perked up. "Today is not about him," she thought. Today was about her walking in obedience to what God has assigned her to do. With that in mind, she entered the sanctuary with her head held high. Not caring about who knew her news. She knew who she was in God and that she'd made it right in her heart with him. Even though she was still struggling, she hadn't yielded to temptation and she was determined to keep it that way!

She walked into the back office. Flora was beginning Praise and Worship and the atmosphere was perfect. She was ready to preach. When she walked out of the office and entered the pulpit she saw all of the Pastors, Evangelists, Apostles, and Prophets that she'd helped over the years by doing Praise and Worship or solos were there. That made her feel really good. She looked out into the audience and saw friends, family, church members, participators, spectators and some enemies too. However, of all those people, there was still no Tony.

There was however, someone familiar on the very back wall waving at her and smiling. She couldn't really make out the face because of all of the people there. Oh well, I'll see who that is eventually. It was now time to give. Pastor Dudley stood and gave directions for the people to walk and place there offering in the offering basket. The stranger began to walk towards the front of the church. He was in an all black suit looking very nice with the nice being extended. His hand was the hand that was waving at her from the back. It was Rayne. He smiled at her as he walked past and she waved at him. She felt her heart flutter and wondered if it was the baby causing this reaction or something else.

Following the offering, her Pastor introduced her and called up Rayne Washington to do a solo. He sung, "Stand," by Donnie McClurklin. It brought her to tears. She dried it up because the microphone would be in her hands next. When he finished, he gave her the microphone and took his seat. She gave her honor to God, Pastor Dudley, her parents, siblings and all others in their respective places. She then said a prayer, read her scripture and began her sermon. The entire message was filled with the audience's, "that's right, amen, say so, you better preach Emerald, and umm, that chile is preaching." The whole time that Emerald stood up there she prayed within saying God, if you called me then you'll deliver this word. God did exactly that. So many people testified of needing the words that came from her mouth through the leading of the Holy Spirit. Emerald felt good and gave God all of the glory for it.

After the service people greeted her, encouraged her, congratulated her and thanked her for the message. Rayne came up and she became warm all over. He introduced her to his grandmother and his mother's friend. His mother, Shirley, was there too. They all hugged and kissed her. He said he'd call her later. As soon as Emerald got a break from the hugs, she told her parents that she was going home because she felt lightheaded.

"Emerald," a voice yelled from across the church. She turned around to see who it was. Unfortunately, it was Evangelist Ann Groseby. She was the saint minus the s. She was in everybody's business and it was not because of her being concerned. It was out of sheer nosiness. She loved gossip; she lived, moved and had her being for it.

"Wait up," she screamed. Emerald wished that she'd ignored the sound of her name and kept on walking. "Hey Emm, how are ya?" "It's Emerald and I'm doing fine." "Oh, well excuse me. I was just trying to be friendly." She adjusted her hat that was bigger than her entire body and her body was big! "Anyway, girl what's this I hear about you being pregnant?" Emerald's heart sank. How did she know? She's the queen of news and all but how could she know? She lightly touched Emerald's stomach. Emerald felt fire run through her. "Please don't touch my stomach Ann."

"Well, is it true?" She stepped back to give Emerald a once over look. "Is what true?" "You being pregnant." "Who told you that?" Emerald's hands were in her hips by now and her neck moved with every syllable that she pronounced. People kept knocking them as they walked by them to exit the sanctuary. That aggravated Emerald even more.

"That's not important. The point is if you are then you need to be sitting down in the back of the church somewhere not preaching to anybody. You need to be saved. Uh-uh, bet your parents not putting you up on a pedestal now. Everybody wanna preach!" Ann began to walk away while shaking her head and mumbling to herself. When Emerald looked around there was an audience. All eyes were literally on her. Ann noticed it to and stopped in her tracks. She turned around then to see who else would jump on Emerald. She loved drama! She was wearing a smirk on her face than Emerald so eagerly wanted to snatch off.

"You know Ann, I've been accused of many things but one of the things that no one could accuse me of being is a liar. With that being said, Yes, I am pregnant."

Sounds of shock filled the air. Emerald turned and faced the audience. She saw a look of pleading in her parent's eyes but she continued anyway. "I am pregnant. I made a mistake. The mistake that I made however, is not what I'm carrying on the inside of me." She caught Pastor Dudley's eyes and he looked proud. Ann folded her

arms and leaned against the wall. She
looked like she'd done the world justice by
exposing Emerald's secret but God had
something in store for Ann!

"The mistake that I made was when I
committed fornication. I've repented to God,
to my parents and to my leader. I'm free.
Now if any of you have something in your
heart because of how you think things
should be then you might want to consult
God quickly. Because technically, I don't
owe you all or anyone else an explanation
but I gave you one anyway." Marcus
wrapped his arm around Emerald. "Let's
get you home baby." They turned to walk
away and Louise was right behind them. So
many emotions filled the air.

"Wait a minute," a male voice shouted. It
was Phillip, a guitarist from a nearby
church. Everyone turned to see what he
wanted. Marcus walked to him in a daring
way that Emerald had never witnessed
before. She was a little bit frightened at her
father's mannerism. "May I help you with
something Phillip?" "No you can't but Ann
can." Marcus and everyone else turned to
look at Ann in order to figure out what
Phillip was talking about.

"Ann how are you going to bring this baby
out like that?" Ann was no longer leaning

on the wall. Her hands were in her hips and her eyes were telling Phillip that she was going to kill him. "Phillip what are you talking about? She shouldn't be preaching to anybody! I don't care what she says."

"You know what Ann," Emerald interrupted. "No Emerald, I've got this," Phillip interjected. He made his way to Ann and she looked like she saw a ghost. "Don't do this Phillip. You'll regret it. I'll see to it." Marcus pulled up a chair for Emerald to sit down. Several people took their seats as well. This was getting good.

"Don't do what Ann? Don't tell the people that you and I have been sleeping around for years? Don't tell them how we've been in the park on the benches, in the back of your car and my car on the dirt roads? Don't tell them how we've been to Motel 6 so much that they know our names," Phillip questioned? Ann hauled off and slapped him.

"How dare you tell lies on me. You wish that happened. You were after me before my husband past." "Yes I was and you never denied me either!" She tried to slap him again but he caught her wrist this time.

"Ann your birthmark is on your left thigh right next to your bikini line." She struggled but he wouldn't let her go. You have a wart under your right breast that irritates you, that why you wear your bra so loose." "Stop it Phillip," she screamed. "You have no right!"

"I don't huh Ann?" "For years you've been the church bully, the pugh pastor. You're always in somebody's business. You, out of all of these people should not be pointing fingers at anybody. I'm married, my wife had her suspicions about us but now she'll know the truth. You're a woman and you never thought about how my wife would feel. You wanted a married man and you slept with a married man while you were preaching and wearing those big hats. The bible refers to a woman like you as a harlot." Phillip giggled while he called her a harlot. He saw Ann for the devil that she was.

"Ann don't you think you owe Emerald an apology, Pastor Dudley asked?" He walked over and released Phillip's grip of her. She rubbed her wrists and looked around the room. "I guess, I'm sorry," she mumbled. "I'm in my fifties and people think that when you past forty-five that you don't have needs. But I have needs too. When my husband was living he was a good man. But I always needed more. Phillip brought me that more. It was wrong I know but no one saw what I was doing. Nobody knew. I figured if nobody knew then nobody could get hurt. Now fifteen years later, here we are." She took off her hat and patted her hair. Her eyes were wet with tears. "I'm sorry Emerald, really I am. I guess I was excited to know that I wasn't the only one in sin."

"But Emerald's not in sin," Pastor Dudley interrupted. "She's made her peace with God. Now it's your turn. I'll need to meet with you tomorrow in my office. Call me in the morning for the time that I'll be available." "Yes sir," she whispered. "All right people it's been a long day let's go home," Pastor Dudley said.

The room was far from quiet as the exited the building. So much had come of the night. Two women and one man were liberated. Two were willingly and the other wasn't but they were all free.

On the drive home, she shed tears again. Evang. Ann hurt her with her outburst tonight. However, these tears were tears of joy. She'd entered into another realm in her life. She gave birth spiritually. She wondered if all of the tears that she shed the past few weeks would compare to the tears that might be shed the next few months.

Somehow, she knew that better days were coming.

CHAPTER 16

When she walked up the stairs to her apartment, she could hear her phone ringing. She hurried to answer it. "Hello, Hello," she said hoping the person hadn't hung up? "Hey Lady." "Hey Rayne, what's up?" "Girl I didn't know you had a holler in you like that!" She laughed and said "whatever Rayne." "I didn't see your man there or did you just not introduce me to him?" "He wasn't there Rayne." "Wow, what excuse could he have for not being there? This was the biggest day of your life. I drove all the way from California to be here and he's right in Charleston and couldn't come. Man, I'm sorry Emerald but your boy is trifling. I wouldn't even call him a man," Rayne continued angrily. Emerald interrupted, "Thank you for coming Rayne. You did a beautiful job with the song. I hate to be rude but I really have to go now, good-bye." Without waiting on a response, she hung up the phone.

She was angry with Rayne. She was angry with Tony and she was angry with herself. She was only angry with Rayne because he said everything that she didn't want to hear. But the fact of the matter was that it was all the truth.

CHAPTER 17

It was 11:54pm and Emerald thought she heard the phone ringing. It woke her from a deep sleep. She grabbed the telephone. "Hello," she said in a groggie voice. "Hello," she said again but there was nothing but a dial tone. She heard the ringing again and realized that it was her doorbell and not her telephone. Without putting on a robe she ran to the door wearing nothing but a champagne colored, silk negligee that clung to her all too well. "Who is it," she asked as she approached the door? "It's Tony," the person ringing the bell said. With fear that something was wrong, she hurriedly unlocked the door and opened it. "Hey are you ok," she asked sounding worried? "Yeah why?" "Well, because you've never come to my house this late before." She hit the light switch and closed the door behind him.

Tony's eyes filled with lust. Emerald still hadn't realized that she was standing there half-naked in her bedclothes. "So what's up Tony?" "You tell me, standing there looking sexy as ever." He licked his lips and looked her up and down. Emerald looked down and noticed her attire. She tried to cover herself but did not succeed. She began to walk away while saying, "Let me get my bathrobe, Tony. I'll be right back." He grabbed her by the wrist and pulled her to him. "What are you doing," she asked angrily? He began to kiss her. He kissed her cheeks, her ear and the corners of her lips. She was struggling to get away from him so he kissed whatever portion he could get to. She tried to push him away but he'd backed her into the wall and she couldn't move. He was so much stronger than she was. He removed his mouth from hers. "I want you so bad right now," he said as he kissed her neck and ears. He was determined to have her tonight. She was determined that he wouldn't!

Suddenly, Emerald had a flash of her standing in the front of the congregation and preaching, "You can have life in the spirit, if you kill the flesh." With strength that came from within she pushed Tony so hard that he stumbled over the coffee table and fell while screaming obscenities.

"What's your problem," Tony asked seeming to look like the devil himself? "My problem is the fact that you weren't there tonight. And for a while you haven't been there," Emerald said as she paced in front of him with her hands on her hips. "This was the most important night of my life and you were a no show. Then at almost midnight, you come ringing my doorbell because you want sex! Just get out Tony."

Emerald walked to the door to open it. "Come on with that man. I wouldn't come here just for sex. I came by here to spend time with you." "Spend time with me! Are you serious? You must really take me for a fool! Where you should have been spending time was at church tonight." "Emerald I was looking for a job," Tony said, looking more pathetic then he sounded. "You were looking for a job?" "You must think that I'm stupid or something. It's Sunday. My program started at five and ended at seven thirty p.m." Tony tried to speak but Emerald continued. "You couldn't give up two and a half hours of your day. Tony get out now!"

"Fine then, I'll leave," Tony said angrily. "I'll tell you what though, I won't be at the next doctor appointment. As a matter of fact, it doesn't make sense for me to be at any of them. You can call me when the baby is born or if you change your mind about the abortion."

"You know what Tony, I hate you to the tenth power! You don't have to come to the doctor and I won't be calling you about an abortion because I am having this baby! We will do even better without you," she said pointing in his face. " I mean," she said with her hands in her hips, "I should've seen this coming." Tony gathered his things while Emerald talked. He stood in the doorway. She placed one hand on the opened doorknob. "You have absolutely nothing to offer me." Tony stepped dead in his tracks as if he were mesmerized and confused. Emerald had never stood up to him like this before. "You're not saved and you're not even trying to get saved. You don't even have a job." Tony tried to interrupt but she wouldn't let him. She kept talking. She was determined to just let it all out! "You're a grown man who would rather collect workman's compensation than to get your rusty behind out there and work. My job takes very good care of me. The furniture that you see, I own it. That car outside is mine. You drive a rental and the rental company is looking for you as we speak. The furniture company is threatening to repossess your living room set. Tony couldn't make a donkey look good. You're a disappointment to the family of donkeys. As far as I'm concerned Tony you don't exist." With that, she slammed the door in his face.

She ran and jumped on her bed, looked around the room and fell over laughing. She laughed so hard that tears spilled from her eyes and she was coughing too. Her laugh was a laugh of liberation. She'd been liberated from the counterfeit of a husband.

She was free. She was free of worry and free of the what-ifs concerning Tony. She was now prepared and ready to live a life of happiness again. She was a single, pregnant, preacher but she was right with God!

CHAPTER 18

About two months has passed since she'd last talked to Rayne. He was on her mind a lot lately. She decided to call and check on him. She dialed his number and was disappointed when the operator said, "The number you have reached is not in service." Her heart seemed to break in two pieces. "Oh well, maybe it just wasn't meant to be," she thought. She rubbed her stomach, which was quite round and large. She was now approximately four and a half months pregnant. She loved the way she looked. She was extremely beautiful. Her hair was growing, nails were as long as claws and her skin was flawless. She was due for another ultrasound next week to determine the gender of the baby. However, right now she had to determine how she would move all of the boxes into her new apartment by Saturday. She'd found a nice two-bedroom apartment on the other side of town. It was a lot closer to her job which was a plus. She'd packed almost everything but now she just needed to move it. Her brothers, uncles and her father would be there to help her. She was just ready to go. The apartment held too many memories of her past. It was only Thursday, so on tomorrow evening the moving process would begin.

Friday evening came quickly. Boxes were quickly being lifted and put into the cars and trucks. She was so grateful for the help. Her mind went into thinking of Rayne again and just as it did, her phone rang. "Hello. Hello is anyone there?" She heard crackling in the phone as if they were on a cell or a payphone. But she was becoming irritated anyway. "Hello," she said again. "Hey Lady." Emerald almost fell over when she heard his voice. Just as the devil sent Tony across her path, God was sending Rayne across hers as well. The funny thing is, he was sending him all along but Emerald kept passing him by.

"Hey Rayne. I was just thinking about you," Emerald said cheesing like a Cheshire cat. "You, thinking about me, it must be about to rain!" Emerald laughed at Rayne's comment. "Don't say that Rayne, I'm moving. The last thing that I need is for it to rain." "Moving, where to?" "Across town. Rent went up and I wasn't trying to pay it." "I can understand that. If you can come and get me I'd be glad to help. My car isn't available right now. My sister took my car to go and run an errand." "Thanks Rayne but my car is loaded with stuff and besides,

we're almost done. But I really do
appreciate the thought." "No problem."
"What are you doing later Rayne?"
"Nothing, just chilling with my homeboys.
Why? What's up?" "Nothing, I was just
wondering if you wanted to come by later?
I can give you the address," Emerald
offered. "Ok Emerald, it must be about to
storm if you're inviting me over!" "Ha, ha,
ha. Rayne." "No, foreal though Emerald,
I'm not sure how late I'll be so I'll call you
and let you know." " Alright, talk to you
later Rayne, Bye."

Emerald was bubbling over with excitement.
Why was she so excited about Rayne? For
almost four years he was just a guy that
would not leave her alone even if she paid
him to. And now, she didn't want him to
leave her alone. But she wouldn't dare tell
him how she felt.

At ten o' clock that night everything was
moved and unpacked. The process of
moving out the old apartment went by
quickly. Flora had her movers and Emerald
had hers. Emerald was officially on her
own. The new apartment smelled of fresh
paint and cardboard boxes. She had a great
window view of the area. Her window's
length went from the ceiling to the floor.
She opened her blinds and took in the
scenery. Across from her living room sat

other apartment buildings. To her right was the office, pool and laundry room area. To her left were more apartments. Colorful plants were everywhere. Palm trees decorated the entire parking area. Whoever did there landscaping knew what they were doing completely. The lights bouncing off of the pool area made it look very inviting.

Emerald walked towards her bedroom. On the way there she admired her dining room and coat closet that sat on the opposite side of her living room. Down the hall on the right was her kitchen. It was made just for cooking and nothing else. It was equipped with a beige colored stove and refrigerator, stained wood cabinets trimmed in gold and a beige colored dishwasher. The sink was silver with glass water faucets. She leaned against the wall and smiled. Across from the kitchen would be the baby's room. It was huge. She'd placed her desk and computer against the window to block out burglars. The desk was huge enough to cover most of the window. So if someone tried to break in, they'd hurt themselves more than anything else in the process. The bedroom had a huge walk-in closet that held some toys and books that Emerald had already purchased for her unborn child. She looked around the room and momentarily daydreamed about where the crib would be and what color scheme she would use. She imagined herself sitting in the rocker with a huge handmade quilt draped over her and the baby while she sang and rocked the baby to sleep. She smiled peacefully and left the room. When she stepped out of the bedroom and back into the hallway she noticed the guest bathroom. It was a full bath, which pleased Emerald because that meant that any guest who stayed over would have their own bathroom to use and wouldn't have to use hers. Emerald was very territorial and private about certain things. Her bedroom and bath were two of them.

Down the hall was Emerald's master bedroom. It had a large window as well, in which she pushed her dresser up against. It stood directly in the middle of the window. She placed her Queen sized bed against the other side of the room in a diagonal position. Directly to the right of the dresser was Emerald's closet. It was a walk-in but someone had built shelves in it. This made Emerald very happy because she had a million and one pairs of shoes it seemed like. Emerald kicked off the shoes that she was wearing and stepped into the plush caramel colored carpet that adorned the apartment floor. She felt like she was walking on clouds. She went over to her bed and laid on it. She looked at the clock on the wall that sat in the belly of a porcelain doll. It read 10:15pm.

"I guess Rayne isn't going to call," she disappointedly said to herself. She was use to being disappointed by men that she dated so this wasn't a surprise to her at all. She wearily lifted herself off of the bed and decided to grab a bite to eat and hit the sack. Once again when she was about to give up, the phone rang, and yes, it was Rayne. "Hello." "Hey Lady, please forgive me. I got tied up and I'm just getting to the place where I could call you." "That's ok," Emerald sighed still feeling disappointed. "I guess we'll have to reschedule or did I just blow my chances?" "No, of course you haven't blown your chances," Emerald smiled and said. "We can definitely reschedule." "Ok, well I'll call you tomorrow then." "Ok, Rayne." Tomorrow couldn't get there fast enough.

CHAPTER 19

When Emerald awoke she prepared herself some breakfast, prayed and then called Rayne. He said that he would call her but she couldn't wait any longer. She looked over at the clock. It was 8:30 on a Saturday morning. "He is going to kill me for calling this early," she thought. "Hello," Rayne answered half asleep. "Oh God he sounds so sexy," she thought to herself. She imagined him shirtless, pants less and under those warm covers. "Ooh, if I could just be there with him!" "Girl stop thinking that way. Get yourself together," her innerman said. "Hello," he repeated. "Hey sleepy head." "Hey Lady, what's up?" "Nothing, I woke up with you on my mind and figured that I would go ahead and give you a call. I know you said that you'd call me but I guess I beat you to the punch." "That's no problem. You have to make up for all of the times that I've called you and acted like you were busy or walking out of the door or something." "I know Rayne, bad Emerald," she said as she slapped herself on the hand. Rayne was wide-awake now. He sat up in bed and rubbed his eyes.

"Listen Emerald I need to tell you something." "Ok, what is it." "You're probably not going to want to hear this but, I love you man. I always have. Nothing will ever change that but I've been after you for four years now. You need to make up your mind about what we are to each other." "Rayne you don't love me," Emerald said as she lounged on the love seat in her bedroom that sat at the foot of her bed. "What you love is the chase. You only want me because you can't have me."

"Emerald that's not true. I'm in love with you. You're all I think about. It's been four years Emerald. What man do you know would chase you for four years without loving you?"

"Ok fine, you love me, then tell my mother that. If you can get pass my parents then you can get pass anybody." "I'll tell your mama that I love you. I'm not scared of her or your daddy." "Ok, Mr. Big Stuff, hold on for a minute."

She clicked the phone and called her mother, Louise, on three way. "Hello." "Hey mom." "Hey boo, how you feeling?" "I'm good. Mom listen I have Rayne on the phone with us on three way." "Who?" "Rayne mom, the guy that sung at my initial sermon." "Oh Ok. Hi Rayne," Louise said remembering who he was. "Good Morning Mrs. Louise." "Mom, Rayne has something to tell you." "Ok, Rayne what is it?" "What do I have to tell your mom," Rayne playfully asked? "You have to tell my mom what you just told me." Emerald wasn't playing at all! "Ok, fine that's no problem. Mrs. Louise, I'm in love with your daughter. I've been chasing her for four years now and I'm tired. She won't give me the time of day and I'm fed up." Emerald sat on the other end of the phone speechless and shock. She couldn't believe that he'd actually done it. No man has ever told her parents that they loved her before. He must really be serious. But she was determined to drag it out. Her mouth was open and she felt a drop of drool hit her chin and wiped it quickly. She was grateful that no one was there to see her facial expression. Louise on the other hand was laughing hysterically. " I can't believe you all called me with this." Emerald didn't think it was funny at all. "You know what Rayne, I've always liked you. I could never remember your name but I always loved to hear you sing," Louise said still chuckling at the situation.

"Yes mam, Rayne said humbly." "Man, Mrs. Louise, on the real though. Your daughter is hard." "All right Rayne," time to go Emerald interrupted. "No," Rayne interrupted, "you wanted me to talk to your mother so now I'm talking." Emerald was surprised at his boldness. "Rayne I'm not playing, I'm going to hang up." "So, hang up." "My number's in the phonebook Rayne. You can call me back if she hangs up!" Louise was having too much fun with this. Emerald was once again speechless. Her mother and her friend were ganging up on her. She realized that she'd walked herself into this so she just sat back and rolled with the punches. When Louise realized that Emerald had nothing to say, she continued speaking. "Alright Rayne, tell me all about it."

"Man, Mrs. Louise I've tried everything, flowers, cards, calling her, trying to take her out and still she won't give me a chance. She likes those rough neck dudes. The ones that don't mean her no good. Mrs. Louise would you believe she had the nerve to tell me that I'm too nice?" "No she didn't." "Yep, she sure did." "I mean, Mrs. Louise, I'd give my life for your daughter. My family and friends knew how I felt about her. I couldn't keep a relationship with no other woman, they even know how I feel about her." "Whoa," was all Louise could say." "I'm tired man. Then she's gonna turn around and tell me that I don't love her." "You don't love me," Emerald interjected, "you just love the chase I already told you that." "Emerald how are you going to tell me how I feel? You're not in my brain."

"Ok, ok children," Louise said breaking up the argument and laughing at the same time. "Rayne, I'll tell you what. Why don't you come to church with us tomorrow and then come over for dinner and we'll see what happens?" "Oh my God, Mom did you just invite him to our church and our home?" "No, I invited him to our church and my home." Emerald rolled her eyes. "And don't be rolling your eyes at me either Emerald." Emerald smiled and shook her head at her mother's x-ray vision. This time

Rayne was laughing hysterically. He paused
long enough to say, "Mrs. Louise I'd love to
come. What time should I be there?"
"Service starts at 11am." "Ok, I'll see you
there." "Good-bye Mom," Emerald
sarcastically said. "Bye," her mom said
while laughing and disconnecting the call.

"Hello," Emerald said while clicking back
over to Rayne. "Uh-uh, I have mama on my
side," Rayne playfully said. "So, she's not
the boss of me." They both laughed. "Well,
I guess I'll see you tomorrow," Emerald
said. "Sho nough." They both hung up the
phone with the brightest smile they'd had in
a very long time and it was because of the
pleasure they gave each other just knowing
that the other is there.

CHAPTER 20
Church was jumping when Emerald got
there. She wore a brown dress that came to
her ankles with a brown top that had fur
around the collar. Gold accessories adorned
the outfit along with brown pumps to match.
She was pregnant but still a no joke when it
came to looking good. When she arrived
Rayne was already there. Along with him
came his mother and his grandmother. His
mother, Shirley, always loved Emerald. No
one ever seemed to be able to compete with
her. Emerald's being pregnant didn't bother
Shirley one bit. She just wanted them to be

together as did his entire family. She
wanted it however, not only because she
liked Emerald but also because the Lord told
her the first time that she met her that she
would be Rayne's wife. She was simply
holding fast to what God had spoken into
her spirit.

When Rayne saw Emerald his eyes lit up.
She waved and took her seat. She sung
along with the choir as they sung, "*I've Got
the Victory*, v-I-c-t-o-r-y." Pastor Dudley
preached a fiery sermon and the altar was
packed with people when the sermon was
over. Ten people gave their lives over to
Christ and the church really went to praising
God then. The bible says that the angels
rejoice over one soul but they had ten to
dance about. Emerald watched Rayne, sing,
wave his hand and even dance a little as the
souls came to Christ. She always wanted a
man that didn't mind loving God and
expressing that love because if he could
express his love to Christ then assuredly he
could express his love to her! The
benediction was said shortly after and her
father ended with the oh so famous song,
"*Let everybody say, Amen, amen, amen.*"

After service, she went and greeted Shirley
and Rayne's grandmother with a hug and
kiss on the cheek. She hugged Rayne last
and felt his hand linger on her back as if

they were a couple, which they weren't.
However, she couldn't bring herself to
remove his hand. It just felt right being
there. "Emerald you look so pretty," Shirley
commented. "She sure does," Rayne said
and kissed her cheek. Emerald felt herself
blushing and prayed that it wasn't
noticeable. As they left out of the sanctuary
Emerald received one hundred of –"who's
that with you, he's cute, is that your baby's
daddy, so forth and so on." Of course,
Emerald didn't reply to anything that was
said to her. She took Rayne's hand in hers
and they entered there cars and left.

Rayne followed her to Louise's house.
When they got inside they all took their
seats in the family room. "Ooh some of
them folk are nosey," Rayne said. "Yeah,
some of them are but most of them are ok
though." "Yeah but I can tell that they love
you Emerald." Maybe nosey is the wrong
word, they're just protective," Rayne said
and nodded his head at the same time.
"True, Emerald agreed but some of them are
still nosey though." They laughed together.
"Alright yall come to the table and let's eat.
I'm starving," Emerald's younger brother,
Demetrius yelled.

They all gathered around the table.
Emerald's father asked Rayne to bless the
food and they all dug in. No one brought up

why Rayne was there or what was going on with him and Emerald until the dessert came to the table.

"So Rayne, what's the deal with you and my daughter," Marcus asked? "Well sir, I love your daughter. I've loved her for quite sometime now." Rayne glanced at Emerald and she saw the love in his eyes. Marcus paused for a moment because he and everyone else saw it too. It wasn't just lust this time like the other men that came after his daughter felt. And who could blame them. She was simply beautiful. But Marcus decided that he couldn't let him off the hook that easy.

"Oh really, and what exactly do you love about her?" "I love everything about her." "Everything is a broad statement son, can you break it down into more specific terms?" "I love her smile. I love her heart. I love that she loves God. She's giving, caring and kind. She's a clean woman. She keeps a clean house and you don't find that often in women her age nowadays. She's a lady and she's not easy!" "Not easy, what do you mean?" "Well, it's been four years and she won't give me the time of day. She presents a challenge and I like that. I wish it didn't take four years but we've become very good friends in the process." "Ok, so then what are your intentions with her?"

"Sir, I'd marry your daughter today if she'd say yes. I love your daughter. She's my wife, I know she is." "So you're saying that you'd marry my daughter today?" "Yes sir I am." "What about the baby?" "When Emerald told me that she was pregnant I told her that I wished it were mine. Not that I wished we'd slept together or anything." Rayne held his hand up and laughed a little. Everyone at the table chuckled at him backtracking himself and being careful of his every word to Emerald's father. Marcus wasn't smiling at all. "But Sir, Emerald is going to be a mother and I will love her and that baby with all of my heart if she'll let me." Rayne looked at Emerald in a pleading way. "But, I understand that she's already taken." "Ok," was all Marcus said and he too looked at Emerald. The look in Marcus eyes let Emerald know that he was pleased with Rayne. No one brought up Tony and Emerald was so glad they didn't. She still hadn't told Rayne that it was over between them.

After dinner and light conversations they decided to leave and head home. "What are you doing later," Rayne asked Emerald as he walked her to her car? He closed her car door behind her and watched her put her seatbelt on. She put her window down and answered him. "Going home and chillin out." "True." Rayne held his head down and played with the rocks on the ground with his feet. Emerald sensed that Rayne wanted to ask to spend more time with her. "Would you like to come over and watch a movie or something?" He didn't respond but continued to look towards the ground. "Rayne." He lifted his head and smiled. "Yeah, that's cool." "Ok, you can follow me."

When they entered the apartment, Rayne looked around and admired how neat and nicely decorated it was. "Rayne you can have a seat, I'm gonna go and get out of these clothes." Rayne's mind quickly wandered to her being naked and he had to bring himself back. When Emerald came back she was wearing a red t-shirt and a pair of blue sweatpants. Her feet were covered in Winnie the Pooh socks. "Emerald do you mind if I take off this shirt and tie? I have a t-shirt on underneath." "Sure that's fine." She took a seat next to Rayne and turned the television on. She put the volume on low so they could talk for a while. Rayne watched her facial features and admired how beautiful she was. He wished they were married so he wouldn't be restricted to just sitting on the couch with her and behaving himself. Emerald glanced over at Rayne and sighed.

"Rayne, we need to talk." Her words knocked him out of his trance. "Oh, ok what's up?" She adjusted herself slightly in order to face him. "Rayne, Tony and I are no longer together." Rayne had to fight the smile that wanted to creep up on his face. "Why?" "What happened?" "He wants me to have an abortion and I refuse to. So the engagements off and so is our relationship. He will not be having a part of this child's life either."

"Do you still love him?" Rayne had to breathe because he was not prepared to hear her say yes. He wanted her to love him not some other man. "Right now Rayne, I'm praying that God would help me not to hate him. So the answer to your question is no, I don't still love him." Rayne smiled and held his head down while tapping on the sofa.

"I have something for you Emerald." He pulled an envelope out of his bible and placed it on the couch between the two of them. She opened it and inside was a letter addressed to her. She placed it on the coffee table and looked over at the television. He placed the letter back on her legs and told her to open it. "You want me to read this now?" "Yep." The letter was approximately four pages long and it basically restated what he'd already told her. It said that he loved her, wants her to marry him and allow him to help her raise this child but that he wasn't waiting any longer. If she couldn't give him an answer, not only would he not chase her anymore but he would end their friendship, permanently.

CHAPTER 21

Emerald had no words. He'd watched her the entire time that she read the letter trying to gather what her movements meant but to no avail, he got nothing. Emerald, however, was a great actress. The room seemed to close in around her. He had been there for her for the past four years. The letter was four pages long and just as it ended, there four-year friendship might end as well. She looked into his hopeful eyes and for the first time she couldn't imagine being without him.

She folded the letter and placed it back into the envelope. She placed her hands on her lap and adjusted in the seat again. She sighed and said, "Ok." "Ok as in you'll give me a chance?" "Ok as in we can hang but I need time. I love you as a friend but I've just been hurt Rayne. I don't want to date you on the rebound. So can we see each other as friends and allow me to heal?" She didn't see much hope in his eyes, only disappointment. "If it turns into something more I promise that I won't run from it." "I need more than that Emerald!" He began gathering his things as if preparing to leave. "Don't you at least see it turning into something more?" She looked away from him to hide the tears in her eyes. He'd never seen her cry before and she didn't want today to be that day. She stood and walked towards the window. Rayne threw his things on the couch realizing that if she needed another four years that he wasn't going anywhere. If God said it then that's all he needed. And he knew that God said it! He heard her sniff and approached her from behind. He turned her to face him and she quickly dropped her head to hide her tears. He lifted her chin with his fingers and kissed her damp cheek. He pulled her to him and placed his chin on top of her head. They hugged tightly for a while without saying anything. She just weeped in his arms.

He pulled her away so that he could look at her. "Emerald, I'll give you as much time as you need if you promise not to push me away anymore. You deserve to be loved Emerald. All I want is to give that love to you. I want to make you happy." Tears continuously flowed from her eyes and her heart. She so badly wanted to reach out to him but she just couldn't.

Sit down Emerald. She sat down on the sofa and he sat down next to her. "Emerald, I was engaged a few months ago." She looked up in shock. "I was settling for someone else because I knew that you wouldn't have me. I didn't even ask to her to marry me. She told me we were getting married and started planning the wedding." Emerald smirked. "My family wouldn't even come to the wedding because I wasn't marrying you." "What?" "Ok Rayne, now you're lying." "If you don't believe me then call my mother and ask her." "Dial the number," Emerald said daringly. She didn't think that he would really dial the number. "No problem." Rayne dialed the number. "Hello," his mother answered. Once again, Rayne had called her bluff. "Hi, Mrs. Shirley, this is Emerald." "Hi, Emerald." "Mrs. Shirley, Rayne told me to call you and ask you why no one was coming to his wedding from your family." "We weren't coming because we knew that girl wasn't his wife. Yall are supposed to be together and we wanted no part of it. We know what God said." "Ok," Emerald said slowly and in astonishment. I guess that answers my question so I'll talk to you later." "Ok Emerald, Bye."

"Now do you believe me?" "I guess so. But Rayne, I'm pregnant with someone else's baby. He didn't want me so why would you?" Emerald and Rayne were both shocked at her blunt question. "He didn't want you because he wasn't ordained for you. I, however, was ordained for you and you for me over two thousand years ago. We fit together like a hand and glove. You are my rib." He took her hand in his. "Emerald you're the missing part of me. I can never be complete without you. And this baby is my baby. I don't care if you slept with someone else. This baby has a new DNA."

"Ok, Rayne. I'll give you a chance but we have to take it slow." "You have my word baby." He kissed Emerald on the forehead and then bent lower to kiss her stomach. "Hey Lil Rayne, Daddy's home." Emerald laughed and hugged his neck when he stood up. "I'm glad you're here Rayne." "Me too. So when is the next doctor's appointment? I don't want to miss a thing if I can help it. He threw his hands up in the air. Hold up, am I moving too fast?" "No, your straight, we actually have an appointment this Thursday at 10am." "Here's the address," she said while she gave him a card with the address on it. She took a seat because she was beginning to feel tired. "Alright well if I'm in town then I'll be there but I'll call you if I can't make it."

He stood and prepared to really leave this time. He knew that a movie was out of the question now. Emotions were running high and even though they had no paper behind it or a ceremony he felt like he was already married to Emerald. Therefore he wanted to do married people things. Instead he looked at her and said, "Well, I'd better be going." "The hours getting late and you and my baby needs rest." She blushed and got up off of the sofa with him. He headed for the door. "Do you have money for yourself? Do you need anything?" "No, I'm fine thank you." Emerald had never had a man check to make sure that she had money before other than her father so it left her a little baffled. "Alright, well if you need anything at you call me ok." "Ok." He kissed her cheek again and left. It had been a long time since Emerald felt this way about anyone and it felt so good.

CHAPTER 22

On Thursday Emerald dressed in some black slacks with black boots and a red wrapped blouse. She wore a silver dangling earring and necklace set. She graced her lips with a burgundy colored lipstick and her eyes with black eye liner and mascara. She put on her black leather coat and headed for her appointment. She looked good!

She hadn't heard from Rayne so she figured that he'd probably meet her at the doctor's office. When she got to her car, Rayne was leaning on it with a card in his hand. She smiled and sighed a sigh of relief when she saw him. "Good morning Lady," he said as he walked towards her for a hug. "Rayne, what are you doing out here?" She turned her head so he could kiss her on the cheek. He pulled her to his car. "I'm taking you to your appointment." "Why didn't you come in?" "I wanted to surprise you." "Oh, that's so sweet." "Are you ready to go?" "Yes." "Well, come on, I have my car nice and warm for you." He opened the door and watched her slide in his car. He reached in and locked her seatbelt for her. She could smell his cologne and it stirred something inside of her. He closed her door and she reached over to open his door for him. "Wow." "What is it," Emerald asked? "That's the first time any woman has done that for me. Thank you." "Your welcome." "Are you hungry?" "No, I'm fine." They headed to the doctor's.

They arrived at the doctor's office and the nurse quickly asked them to come to the room with the ultrasound equipment. "Do you want me to come with you or just wait here?" She didn't reply but she gently pulled his hand and they walked behind the nurse. "Are you the proud father," the nurse asked as she helped Emerald along the bed? "Yes, I am," he said proudly. Emerald and Rayne looked at each other and smiled. She lifted Emerald's blouse up just below her bra line and scooted her pants down just below her belly button. Rayne adjusted himself in his seat to contain the excitement he felt for the baby and for seeing a glimpse of Emerald's body. He propped his hand on his chin.

The nurse placed the cold blue jell on Emerald's stomach and began to check the baby's heartbeat. When Emerald heard the baby's heartbeat, her heart skipped a beat. She fell in love with the baby right then. The baby rolled over and stuck its thumb in its mouth and began sucking. Emerald called Rayne over and held his hand as they watched the baby move and bounce around on the monitor. The baby opened its legs and there it was. Emerald was having a baby girl. She squealed, laughed and cried at the same time. She was so excited she almost jumped off of the table. Rayne kissed her hand repeatedly as she cried. She was so happy and Rayne was too. "Well maybe we can name her Rayneaetta instead of Lil' Rayne." Emerald popped him on his arm. The nurse cleaned her up and helped her with her clothes. "Are you happy Emerald?" She kissed him on the cheek and said, "More than you'll ever know." Now he was blushing. They spent the rest of the day eating Chinese food and watching movies.

On Friday, Rayne left to go back on the road. When Emerald got in her car to leave for work there was a note on a dashboard. She opened it and read the words written on it, they seemed to leap off of the page, "I LOVE YOU EMERALD, PLEASE DON'T EVER LEAVE MY SIDE! PS, SEE YOU IN A FEW DAYS!" Underneath the note was a box. Emerald decided that she would open it later. If she got any happier she'd fly away. The note brought tears to her eyes. She had a wonderful day at work. She smiled most of the day just thinking about him and what could be in that box. She couldn't imagine what was in it. The anticipation had her giggly all day.

When she arrived at home she went to check her mailbox. She unloaded her bags and made sure to bring the gift box into the house as well. She sat everything down on the dining room table. She sat on the living room sofa and prepared to open the box. It was wrapped in beautiful pink paper and a big white bow. The card read, "To my little girl, Love Daddy." She tore open the wrapping and pulled out a beautiful green and beige memory book. It would be able to hold information from age zero to age five. The inside of it was signed "From, Mommy and Daddy, We Love you" and it was dated. Emerald cried so hard that her blouse looked like she'd been sweating. She called almost everyone that she could think of (those that loved her anyway) to tell them what he'd done. Everyone was so happy for her, especially her mother. When Rayne called her that night she couldn't stop thanking him and telling him how kind he was. He'd made her so happy. One day she'd show him how much.

CHAPTER 23

Months had passed and Rayne and Emerald were still seeing each other. They went everywhere together, church, dinner, breakfast, shopping and he was always the perfect gentleman. His being on the road made things a little difficult at times and Emerald missed him tremendously. His job mainly took him to Illinois and Connecticut. He would be gone for seven to ten days at a time. When Emerald was working, he was working, when she came home, he was asleep in his truck and when she'd got to sleep he'd be awake driving. So they really didn't get to have long conversations until he came home. When he came home, Emerald would leave work just to spend time with him. They enjoyed each other's company around the house whether it was watching nicktoons or having dinner at a five star restaurant. They were happy just being together.

Rayne called Emerald and they talked for about two hours. Just as they were ending there conversation he said to her, "Emerald, I'll be home tomorrow for your doctor's appointment but I'll have to leave the next day. I have a delivery in Charleston and then I have to hit the road again to go back to New York." "Ok well what time will you be in town?" "I'll get in around two in the morning." "Alright well I'll see you just in time for my appointment then." "Yeah, maybe I'll come over and cook for you afterwards." "That would make my day!" "Ok, I'll see you tomorrow, Love you Emerald." "Ok Rayne, Bye." Emerald loved Rayne's cooking. He was in the United States Army for eight years and served as a chef. If you could name it, he could make it. Emerald loved that about him. He was so giving and caring towards her.

Speaking of love, Rayne told Emerald that he loved her quite often. He never ended a telephone call or left her presence without saying 'I love you'. But she would always smile and say ok. She didn't even want to think about uttering those words to another man anytime soon. Emerald had feelings for Rayne but she just wasn't ready to talk about them yet. It was those words and those feelings that caused her to feel so much pain with Tony. She was now seven months pregnant and he had not called, written or come by just as he said and it suited Emerald just fine.

It was the next day. Rayne wrung Emerald's doorbell and she quickly waddled to answer it knowing that it was him. When she opened the door and saw him, she leaped into his arms so fast that she almost knocked him down. "Man baby, are you that happy to see me," Rayne asked while laughing? He was shocked at Emerald's response to seeing him. "Just a little," Emerald replied. She turned on her heels and playfully walked away from him. "Yeah right. Come here and let me see you," he said as he turned her to face him. Ooh, your nose is spreading, Rayne teased. "No it's not," Emerald said while feeling her nose with one hand and playfully hitting at him with the other. He grabbed her hands and kissed her fingers. "Yes it is, the tips are about to reach your ears." "You know what Rayne, you're about to get it." He pulled her into him. "Come here and let me look at you for real." He rubbed her stomach. "You are the most beautiful pregnant woman that I've ever seen. You're just glowing. I love it." Emerald touched his face and kissed his cheek. "Thanks Rayne, now lets get going or we're going to be late."

When they arrived at the doctor's the parking lot was packed. They found a spot in the very back so Rayne offered to pull in front of the office building so she wouldn't have to walk so far. He parked and hurried to her so they could walk in together. Emerald signed into the front desk and sat next to Rayne. He put his arm around her and held her hand with his other available hand. "How are you feeling?" "I'm ok today." "This baby is kicking me like crazy though." He let go of her hand and rubbed her stomach. "Hey daddy's girl, you be still in there." The child became still immediately. Emerald laughed and blushed at the attention that he was giving to her and her unborn child. She was taken aback at the child's response to his voice.

"Ms. Sinclair, the Dr. will see you now," the nurse said. Emerald walked into the doctor's station and took a seat. Rayne sat next to her. They measured her stomach, asked questions, took her weight and it was over.

As promised, Rayne cooked a delicious meal for Emerald. He fried several pieces of flounder, with yellow rice and garden cut green beans on the side. Emerald ate so much that she could hardly move. She propped her feet up on the sofa and pulled a blanket over her. Rayne looked at her in longing. "Would you mind terribly if we lay on the couch and I just held you? No funny stuff, I promise." "It's not that Rayne. I trust you but it's myself that I'm working on." She put her feet back on the ground and sat up on the sofa. "Us lying down together on such close proximity is just too close for comfort." Emerald remembered why she was in this predicament in the first place and didn't want to end up there again without being married. She also remembered how compromising could get you into trouble. In addition to that, she wanted to keep her relationship with God. "You can come and sit next to me though while we watch a movie." Rayne rose from the stand-alone chair and walked over to her. "It would be my pleasure." He sat next to her and watched the movie with only platonic contact but it was killing him to do it.

CHAPTER 24

The next day Rayne prepared to leave to go back on the road. Emerald met him at his truck to see him off. While he loaded everything into the truck Emerald felt her eyes water. He would only be gone for a few days but it seemed like it would be for an eternity. She walked over to hug him and say good-bye. They made small chitchat in the process. She took one of his hands in hers. "So Rayne are you going to miss me?"

"I'll miss you like crazy." They both laughed. "I'm going to miss you too." Rayne had a look of surprise on his face but said nothing. She thoughtfully pulled a lint off of his sweater. She looked at him briefly and saw him lick his lips while looking at her. She thought she'd melt right there in the middle of the street.

"Well I guess I should let you go, Illinois is a far ways from Charleston." "Yes it is," Rayne said while holding his hands behind his back. He felt like if he released them he'd grab her right there and never make it to Illinois but they'd definitely have to make it to the altar- to repent! "Alright, well call me later." "Ok Lady." "I Love You." The words slipped off of Emerald's tongue so smooth but so fast that she shocked herself. "You what," Rayne asked with tears in his eyes. Emerald stepped closer to him, put her arms around his neck with tears covering her face. "I love you Rayne." He literally wept in her arms. She rubbed his back as he buried his face in her neck and tightly wrapped his arms around her waist. "I've loved you for along time. I'm so glad that God placed you in my life and you didn't give up on me when you probably should have." He lifted his head and kissed her slow and tenderly. He looked at her and said, "Wow, Emerald loves me. Emerald loves me. This is going to be a great day!"

What was so funny was that the date was April 1st, which is also known as April fool's Day. However, Emerald wasn't fooling anybody. She loved Rayne more than she'd ever loved before. She knew that he was who God sent to be in her life not only as a friend but also as her husband.

CHAPTER 25

The next few days were incredibly peaceful for Emerald. She'd felt such a release after telling Rayne that she loved him. A few months ago Emerald felt like she'd never be able to love again much less say the words. However, Rayne brought peace and serenity to her life. He carried the love of Christ within him and he was just simply a nice person. Emerald couldn't wait for him to come home. She missed him terribly.

On Thursday, Emerald decided to have lunch at Suntown Dreaming Restaurant with Pamela and Flora. They all drove separate cars and met there at around 1pm. Emerald wore some black stilettos that caused her to walk with pep in her steps. Her head was covered with a pink and black hat and she wore a pink long sleeve blouse with silver buttons and a long black skirt that hung at her ankles. She looked adorable as her seven plus months belly protruded in the

front of her through the blouse. She wore
silver and pink earrings and a long beaded
silver necklace on her neck. Her lips were
brushed with a soft pink lipstick. She was
looking like and felt like a super star! She
always believed in everyone being
confident. Even if she didn't feel confident,
she always looked the part.

When Emerald entered the building she saw
Pamela and Flora in the waiting area. Their
table wasn't quite ready yet. As she walked
over to them the ambiance of the restaurant
enveloped her. Soft jazz played overhead.
Flowers were in a few corners. The bar was
on a separate floor from the rest of the
restaurant. All of the servers wore white
tops with black ties, black slacks, and black
shoes. The ladies all had their hair pulled up
into a ponytail or some type of pinned up
style. The men were close shaven with low
haircuts or if there hair was hung low then
they pinned it up or pony tailed it as well.
The temperature wasn't too hot or too cold
but it was perfect.

"Hey ladies," Emerald said as she hugged
Pamela and Flora and sat next to them.
While they were sitting, Pastor Wates and
Pastor Jones came walking by. Emerald
used to do praise and worship for them when
they'd have revival. She was happy to see
them. But the feelings were not mutual.

"Hey Pamela, hey Flora, they said as they
smiled and hugged them. They looked over
at Emerald and said a cold hi. She didn't
even exist as far as they were concerned.
They looked at her face and then her
stomach as if she had a contagious terminal
disease. The four ladies talked amongst
themselves. Emerald turned her head and
prayed within. She was hurt and astonished
at there treatment towards her. When they
left they said good-bye to Pamela and Flora
but said nothing to Emerald. The buzzer
vibrated and lit up in Pamela's hand to let
them know that there table was ready.

The three of them walked over to the table
and took their seats. The table was round
with a thick white tablecloth on it. In the
middle of the table sat a burgundy, dark
green and off white flowered centerpiece
with vanilla scented candles on each side.
"What will you all be having to drink," the
server asked? They all ordered sweet teas
and the house salad was there meal. Once
the orders were taken Emerald couldn't
resist talking about what just happened.
"Did you all notice anything different about
the way Pastor Wates and Pastor Jones
treated you versus the way they treated me
just now?" "Uh, yeah, sort of," Pamela
hesitantly said wanting to keep peace.
Emerald wanted to keep peace also but she

needed to sort out her feelings and make sure she wasn't hallucinating. "Well, what did you notice?" "They were cold to you because you're pregnant and you're not married." "Um, Um," Flora threw in while sipping on her tea and rolling her eyes at the thought. "Wow, that's crazy," Emerald said with an exasperated look on her face.

"So many people have children out of wedlock. This isn't anything new. I'm not the first and I won't be the last. I still love the Lord but I made a mistake. Should I be treated that way because of it? I mean, was that suppose to be the love of Christ that they just displayed? And as I recall both of them had children before they got married so what gives them the right to hold up there snotty noses at me?"

Pamela and Flora laughed and nodded in agreement. "People are so easy to forget. But that's ok. One day I'll be able to help other women in situations like this." There food came and they said their grace and began to eat. Emerald was quiet and it was obvious that she was upset. "Girl, don't you let those people get to you. You know who you are," Flora said trying to comfort Emerald.

"I'll try but it's hard when the same people whom you helped decide to turn on you because of a mistake. But you know what, God always allows us to see who's for us and whose not. If they really loved me they wouldn't have treated me that way."

"Girl don't worry about Wates, she still has a jerry curl! Now that should be a sin," Pamela said. The table roared with laughter. The remainder of there time together was enjoyable. They finished their meals and went there separate ways.

When Emerald arrived at home she sat on a chair at the dining room table to rest for a few minutes. Her mind wandered back to the incident at the restaurant. She still could not believe the way those Pastors treated her at the restaurant. I've been faithful all these years to God and the church and now because of one bad relationship and fellowship might I add, people are treating me different. These people hugged me all the time and told me that they loved me. Now they treat me like they hate me. They act like I'm a harlot. Is this what the church is really like? Is this what I will have to face for the duration of my pregnancy? Will they treat my child the same way? If I wasn't saved and ran into them today I would probably not ever go to church. Church folks are something else. "Lord help me to be a saint not just a churchgoer," she prayed out loud.

So many questions filtered through her
mind. She put the best on in front of Pamela
and Flora but she was genuinely hurt. What
made her angry was the fact that these two
Pastors had things in there past too. I guess
after entering into Pastoralship they feel like
they are above the law. But God is the
greatest power. No one is above him!

CHAPTER 26
With that thought she arose from the chair
and went into the bedroom to prepare for
work the next day and bible study that night.
While she was in her walk in closet the
doorbell rang. Who could that be? She
dropped the clothing that were in her hands
onto the bed and went to answer the door.
"Who is it she asked on her way there?"
"Your husband," was the reply. "Rayne?"
She walked a little faster and pulled the door
open. When she saw him all of her
problems seemed to disappear. He was
standing there with a white balloon with red
and silver writings on it. It said, 'I love
you'. He also had one red rose in his hand
that played music. "Hey Lady," he said and
handed her the gifts. She jumped into his
arms and kissed him all over is face. "Oh,
I've missed you so much," she said as she
gave him a bear hug. "I've missed you too.
I guess I need to stay away more often if
that's the response I'm going to get." "No

you don't," she said and pulled him into the house. When she closed and locked the door he bent over and kissed her stomach. "Hey Lil Lady, Daddy missed you too." Emerald felt the baby move and knew that she recognized Rayne's voice. Emerald smiled profusely.

"Are you hungry?" "Man I'm starving. What did you cook?" "I haven't cooked anything because I just got home. How come you didn't call me to let me know that you'd be in town today?" "I wanted to surprise you." "Ok well give me about thirty minutes to throw something together." "Well, we can order something I don't want to put you through the trouble of cooking for me." It would be 'my' pleasure. She smiled and walked away.

In the kitchen she prepared fried scallops, brown rice and squash for dinner. Rayne sat in the living room and watched television while she cooked. He looked over at her and admired her youthfulness in appearance but the wisdom of an older woman. Most women her age wouldn't have cooked for him. They may have ordered something but he'd have to pay for it! Emerald, however, was different. She was clean. She always looked and smelled good. He could pop on her at anytime and her house was spotless. She reminded him of his mother because of

that. She was old fashioned. She believed
in cooking and cleaning. She believed in
eating at the table like a family. She
believed in dipping the food on the plate and
serving it to her companion. It was what she
enjoyed doing and because of that he
enjoyed doing it for her as well. They did it
for each other often.

Rayne got up from the couch and stood
behind her. She was so busy that she didn't
even realize that he was standing there until
he kissed the back of her neck. She jumped
and playfully popped him. "Rayne, you
scared me." He laughed. She turned back
around and tended to the food to ensure that
it didn't burn. He hugged her from behind.
Emerald smiled. "I love you so much baby,
you just don't know." Emerald interrupted
his speech by turning slightly and pecked
him on the lips. "I love you too honey."
She moved from his grasp and asked him to
get the plates for her. She felt parts of his
body loving her all too well and she needed
some space.

He handed her the plates and offered to dip
his own food. "No, no, you just have a seat.
I've got this." "Emerald you should really
rest your feet." "I will in a minute I
promise." "Ok," he said. He threw up his
hands in defeat and walked away. Emerald
looked at him over her shoulders and

giggled. He sat at the table while she piled
food onto his plate. He planned on eating
every bite of it too. His mind wandered.
There were things that he'd like to do to
Emerald but she was holy and he reminded
himself of that. Rayne used to be a player.
He would never be with a woman this long
and not get any sexual attention. He'd be
with her but he'd cheat on her too. It wasn't
like that with Emerald. She was the first
woman to 'tame' him and she did it without
even trying. She was all he needed and
wanted. Everyone that knew Rayne also
noticed the change in him and they liked it.
They also liked Emerald because of it. Her
being pregnant didn't make him see her any
different. He admired the fact that she
didn't abort the baby. Most females would
have. He knew a lot of 'church going'
females that did. Never the less, there she
was, facing her first sermon, pregnant, baby
daddy drama, and she kept the baby! An
abortion would have solved all of her natural
problems but spiritually she would have
been dead. She would have been a
malnutritioned preacher. She was happy in
the present state and it showed.

Emerald set Rayne's plate in from of him.
She gave him a fork, knife and paper towel.
She poured freshly made sweet tea with
lemons into his glass of ice. She then took
her seat at the table with him. They held

hands and said the blessings over the food.
"This food looks scrumptious," Rayne said
while stuffing his face. "Um and it taste
even better," he added in. "Thanks." They
made small talk over dinner.

Rayne got up from the table and brought the
balloon and rose over where they were
sitting. "You know, Rayne began, when I
was a little boy I got a kick out of busting
balloons." Emerald started laughing
because he had a mischievous look in his
eyes. "Rayne what are you up to," Emerald
asked while still laughing? Rayne held the
balloon in one hand and a stickpin in the
other. "Would you be mad if I burst your
balloon?" "Yes I would," Emerald replied
more serious this time. "What if I told you
that there was something in it for you?"
"What could be in a balloon for me Rayne?"
"Why don't you burst it and find out?" "But
it's so pretty," Emerald whined. "It's not as
pretty as what's inside," Rayne said.
Emerald's eyes sparkled with exhilaration.
"Ok," she said nervously.

He pulled his chair back and knelt beside her
as she stuck the pin into the balloon. "Why
are you on your knees," she asked as she
watched the balloon deflate? Rayne didn't
respond. He just reached over and ripped at
the balloon. Emerald saw something gold
sitting on the inside but couldn't make out

what it was. She tore the balloon open and inside was her prize. She pulled out an engagement ring. She dropped the remains of the balloon and covered her face with both hands and began weeping immediately. Rayne took her left hand in his and pulled the ring out of the palms of her right hand. He held it out to her. "Emerald, look at me." He reached up and kissed the top of her head. She looked into his eyes in between sobs. "Emerald I bought this ring shortly after I met you four years ago. I always knew that you were suppose to be my wife." Emerald continued to cry. "You are my everything baby and I can't imagine life without you. Will you marry me?" She was crying so hard that she could hardly breathe. "Y-Yes," she said and hugged his neck. "Yes I'll marry you." He laughed and slid the ring on her finger. "I love you Emerald Sinclair." "No sir, that's Emerald Washington." He smiled and kissed her long and hard, savoring every moment.

He pulled her from the dining room table and into the living room. He sat down and placed her next to him. "Do you want to go ahead and set the date," Rayne asked Emerald? "Because when we tell our families and friends they're going to want to know when." "Yeah that's true. I'll get the calendar." She flipped the calendar to a year later. "Whoa, that's too far away," Rayne said. "I've already waited four years and I'm not trying to be engaged that long!" Emerald snickered and said, "Ok when did you want us to get married?" "Definitely before the baby is born. You're almost eight months pregnant now. I want to enjoy the fruits of my labor before your six weeks wait comes once you have the baby." He elbowed her playfully. Emerald hit him on the arm getting exactly where he was coming from. "You are so nasty Rayne." "Seriously Emerald, besides that I want the baby to carry my name."

Emerald looked at him and turned back to there current month on the calendar. It all seemed like a dream to her. He was the perfect man. His only flaw so far was that he was 'too nice' as she always told him. But as she noticed him around other people, he wasn't too nice with them, just her. His love was real and it vibrated from his very being.

"I want to be there when you have the baby with full rights. I don't want any hassles. I want to be able to call you my wife not just my friend." Emerald felt like daring him. "Ok then, let's get married next Saturday," she said jokingly. "That's perfect. How about five in the evening? The weather won't be quite as warm." "Rayne, I was joking." "I'm not. What will we be waiting

on if we wait?" Emerald had no answers.
"Do you really love me Rayne?" She knew
it but she needed to hear him say it one more
time. "I love you so much that I would die
for you Emerald." "Ok then, I guess it's
settled and next Saturday it is." She lightly
kissed Rayne's lips. "See, that's why we
need to hurry up and get married right there!
How much can one man take," Rayne
asked?

Emerald called her parents. They were both
hollering and screaming. They were so
happy for them. "How did he propose,"
Louise asked? Emerald told her the news
detail by detail. "So when is the big day,"
Marcus asked? "Next Saturday." "Next
Saturday," both parents asked in unison?
"Yes. We'll probably just do something
small and private." "Ok, well just let us
know if there's anything that we can do,"
Marcus said. "Thanks Dad we appreciate
that." When she hung up the phone Rayne
was still talking to his family on his cell
phone. They were just as thrilled as her
family was. He hung up and walked over to
Emerald. Before she knew it he'd picked
her up and was swinging her in a circle.
"We're getting married girl." "Yes we are
but for now I think you need to put us (the
baby and I down) being that we just ate,"
Emerald said laughingly. "So let's go ahead
and plan what we're going to do," she said

as he set her feet on the floor. They sat back on the couch and grabbed a notebook and a pen to write with. "So the date is next Saturday at 5:00pm. What will be the wedding colors?" "I don't know!" "That's women stuff!" "How about sage and champagne?" "Yeah, that's nice," Rayne nodded and spoke in total agreement. "What about the guest list," she asked?

The questions went on and on until about three in the morning. They decided to invite only immediate family, close relatives and friends. The ceremony would be held at Mt. New James We Fight for Our Own, Back in the Woods Church at 5:00pm. Pastor Dudley would perform the ceremony. By the time they finished all of the details they were both too tired to move. "Listen Rayne, I would hate for you to get on the road as tired as you are. You can stay here until I leave for work at 6:30." He suddenly woke up! "I can," he said excitedly as he got in a crawling position as if he was about to chase her. "Rayne, I'm not playing with you," she said while laughing. "If you're going to stay then you have to behave yourself." "Ok, ok I'll behave, I promise." "Come on," she motioned to him. Rayne was too tall and too big to lie on the couch. He'd end up falling off. She pointed to the bed. He looked at it, disrobed of his shoes and jumped in.

Emerald went and showered. After the day she'd had she needed the hot water to relax her muscles so that she could sleep well. The three hours that she would get would definitely be needed for work tomorrow. When Rayne heard the shower running the mere thought of Emerald being naked only a few feet away from him made his body stir. "This is going to be a long three to three in a half hours," he said to himself. He knew that he wouldn't get any sleep there. But he didn't want to leave her either. This is another reason why we need to get married soon. I can stand being away from her he continued thinking. She interrupted his thoughts when she came out of the restroom. She spelled like straight strawberries. All he could think of was where is the whipped cream and a marriage license!

Emerald slept in a long t-shirt that came to her knees and she was sure to keep all of her underclothes on. Rayne slept fully clothed but that still didn't stop him from cuddling up to her. Only ten minutes had gone by and he was already trying. "Rayne," Emerald shouted. "What," he shouted back as if he hadn't done anything? Emerald held her giggly belly as she laughed. "Stop playing," she yelled again. He wrapped his leg over hers. "Who said I was playing?" He quickly tucked his face between her neck and shoulder and began kissing her neck and ear. Emerald's body quivered at his touch but she knew that she had to stop him. She wanted there wedding night to be special. "Ok, that's it Mr. Washington." "It's time for you to go home," Emerald said as she pushed at his shoulders for him to move. When he lifted himself off of her she jumped off of the bed. He looked so good lying there. "What did I do," he asked while acting like a

three-year-old boy. "You were being fresh now get out and go home," she said and pointed at her bedroom door with her other hand in her hip. He walked over to her and slid his feet into his shoes at the same time almost falling. Emerald covered her mouth to hide her laughter at him stumbling. "Baby I'm sorry, but we're going to be married in a few days." Emerald tried to comfort him but was still laughing on the inside. "Great, now since it's only a few days then you can wait," she said poking him in the arm. "Alright then Mrs. Soon to be Washington. I'll leave because you and I both know that there's no way I'll be able to lay her next to you for the next few hours and keep my hands to myself." Emerald walked behind him as he headed for her front door. "Ok well call me later," she told him as she saw him off. Emerald shut the door and laughed. "I am going to enjoy being married to him," she thought.

PART
3
TROUBLE
COMETH!

CHAPTER 27

The next day her phone rang non-stop. The word that she was getting married was out. People from her church called all congratulating her and offering to pay and donate things for the wedding. She ended up leaving work and taking the week off just to take care of the wedding. In the midst of the phone ringing, notes and catalogs where everywhere. And to top it all off her doorbell rang constantly too.

However, when the doorbell rang this time, Emerald got a funny feeling in her stomach. She looked through the peephole before she opened the door or even asked who was there. It was Tony. Emerald felt sick. Ding dong, ding dong, he impatiently rang the bell. She slowly opened the door. He had a huge Teddy bear in his hands. "May I help you," Emerald asked as she folded her arms partially across her chest and her huge stomach? Tony got down on one knee. "Oh no, not again," Emerald thought to herself. "Will you marry me Emerald? Be my wife and lets raise this baby together. I was a fool before. I love you. Please say you'll marry me."

Emerald stood in the doorway and noticed the neighbors walking by saying ooh and aah. There responses didn't move her at all and neither did his gesture. She'd repositioned herself with one hand over her mouth and the other on her hip to brace herself up. He looked at her eyes and saw tears. He stood up with hope in his and asked, "baby is that a yes?"

Emerald had been laughing at him the entire time. "You know what Tony, calling you a donkey would be an insult to the family of donkeys. I'm involved and about to be married." His mouth dropped! "Do me a favor and pretend that I never existed. You never knew me. Because as far as I'm concerned simply thinking of you is a waste of my brain cells. Now leave please." She stepped back and reached to close the door. Tony pushed the door open more.

"Are you serious," Tony asked, as his six foot seven inch frame seemed to shrink right before Emerald's very eyes. "I'm as serious as the baby that I have in my stomach that you didn't want!" "Now leave," Emerald yelled. "But Emerald." She pushed and slammed the door in his face and sat on the couch. "That was so nice," she yelled and laughed until she cried. He rang the doorbell a few more times but Emerald didn't even bother to answer.

She called Rayne on the phone and told him what had happened. Rayne didn't find it funny at all. In fact, he felt threatened. He felt like she would change her mind and go back to Tony but he played along and laughed too.

When Rayne came over that evening, Emerald greeted him with a kiss on the cheek and invited him in. She noticed that Rayne wasn't as cheerful as normal. "Why do you look so sad baby?" "It's nothing, I'm straight," Rayne said. "It has to be something. What's going on?"

"This thing between you and Tony has got me worried man." "What thing Rayne? There's nothing between us." Emerald had to sit at the dining room table because she couldn't believe they were even having this conversation. "Emerald this is the second time that he's asked you to marry him. Are you telling me that you didn't even think to say yes to him and end our relationship?" This time she stood; she needed to touch him, to reassure him that she wasn't going anywhere. "No, of course not. Baby I love you."

She walked over and stroked his face with her fingers. The sheer feeling made him tremble. "Rayne, you've been there for me the past four years. You're my best friend. I've fallen in love with you. I don't want Tony or anyone else but you. My only regret is that I didn't say yes to you four years ago." She pecked his lips. "I love you." He smiled, "I love you too." "So I have nothing to worry about," he asked? "Yeah you have something to worry about," she said and backed away. "What's that?" "You have to worry about what were eating for dinner because I'm not cooking," Emerald lightheartedly said. "Girl you are a trip. Come here." She came and he pulled her in for a hug.

His phone vibrated between them and he opened it to see who it was. "It's one of the mothers from my home church." "Hello." "Bless you Rayney Rayne." It was Mother Nelson, a very sweet but at the same time annoying elderly Lady from his church. She'd called him Rayney Rayne since he was a child.

"How you feeling today Mother Nelson?" "Oh I'm making it, this arthritis acts up every now and then and the glasses store can't ever get my scription right but I'm ok darling." "That's good Mother Nelson." "Well boy I hear you getting married?" "Yes mam I am." "Um, um. I hear she's a preacher gal." "Yes man she's a preacher." Rayne took a seat. He had a feeling this would be a while. "Um, um, boy I hear she got a youngin in her belly." "Yes mam, she's pregnant." "Dat your seed?" "Yes mam that's my seed?" Rayne was becoming

annoyed with all the questions and Emerald
was already annoyed at him answering.

"Well tell me dis ya, how she go preach and
she pregnant and ain't got da first husband?"
"Well, Mother Nelson, everybody makes
mistakes. But when God called us he knew
what mistakes we'd make before we made
them. She's gone to the altar and gotten it
right Mother." "But son, you don't think
she need to wait till she has da baby to try to
preach ta somebody?" "No mam. Mother
Nelson, I've known Emerald for over four
years. She's ministered to more single
woman now then she has since I've known
her. I guess this is a situation where God
can turn your mess into a message."

"Alright boy. I guess yall youngins know.
It's a new day we see. Things done change
from my time. But you know I memba
when we friends had youngins in our teen
ages. We still serve da Lord too. I thank ya
here Rayney Rayne. Ya made Motha think
boy. Ya made Motha think. I give yall my
blessing."

"Thank you Motha Nelson. I appreciate
that." "Alright boy, you make sho you come
by and see dis old lady some time here."
"Yes mam. Bye-bye Mother Nelson." "Bye
chile."

"What was that all about?" "That was
Mother Nelson from our church. She heard
that you were pregnant and preaching, She
wanted to make sure that I knew what I was
doing by marrying you. It's all good
though?

"Do you know what you're doing by
marrying me Rayne?" Emerald was feeling
nervous because the situation with Evang.
Ann, the scene at the restaurant and now
this. "Baby, this is the best decision that
I've made my entire life. If I've never heard
from God before I know that I'm hearing
him now."

He walked over and kissed her forehead.
"What do you want to eat Emerald?" She
lightly bit his chin. "How about some good
old fashioned baked beans, beef sausage and
rice?" "That's what's up," he said. He let
her go to enter the kitchen and prepare
dinner. He checked the cabinets for all the
items needed for their dinner and realized
that they had no baked beans. "Emerald I'm
going to go to the store we're out of baked
beans." "Ok." She continued working on
the wedding plans. Just then the doorbell
rang. He opened the door to see who was
there.

"May I help you," Rayne asked? "What's
up dawg? You the brother my woman's

talking bout she gonna marry." Emerald recognized Tony's voice and jumped off of the sofa. "Tony what are you doing here?" He pushed his way through the door and Rayne raised up at him. "You might not want to do that homeboy," Tony said. He pulled out a gun and pointed it at Emerald. "Tony please," Emerald cried. "Tony please, Tony please," he marked her? "Here I am trying to do the right thing by you and this baby and you throwing up in my face that you about to marry this punk." They could smell alcohol on his breath and knew that he'd been drinking. "I'm a punk, man if you were a real man you wouldn't have to come up in here with no gun. That's not changing the way she feels about you."

"Dude you just need to shut up." He pointed the gun at Rayne. "Tony please don't do this. Just tell me what you want," Emerald pleaded with him." "I want you and my baby with me and if you say no then me and this punk will have to live life without the both of you."

"Oh my God, please Tony, stop it." Rayne stood in the front of Emerald. "Look man, we can work something out with you but I'm not going to stand here and let you hurt Emerald or this baby!" Rayne was tall as well so he covered Emerald's entire frame.

"Look, I'm taking Emerald with me," Tony said, "and you aren't going to do nothing about it!" "Try me and see," Rayne said. "No please don't," Emerald said continuing to cry. She felt a contraction and hollered in pain. Her yelling caused Tony to be distracted. Rayne leaped on him and caused the gun to fly out of his hand. Rayne wrestled him to the floor. Emerald quickly walked to the phone to call 911 and inform them of what was happening. "Please guys stop it," she said as she talked to the operator as well. They said that they would send someone over right away.

Emerald rushed back to into the living room. Someone had picked up the gun off of the floor. She saw a glimpse of it as they struggled with each other. Rayne constantly punched Tony in the face every chance he got. Tony's arms were long and he kept missing every time he swung at Rayne.

Emerald saw the footprints vase that Rayne gave to her some months ago. She grabbed it and as soon as she could get a good aim she hit Tony in the head with it. She heard him scream out in pain and then she heard the gun go off. Blood quickly spilled onto the floor. Rayne was still and Tony was trying to move. She yelled out "No, no no no no," while hitting Tony in the head repeatedly for every no she said. "You killed my husband. I hate you." She yelled and hit him until there was no movement at all. She fell to the floor beside them and weeped. How would she make it without Rayne? He was the love of her life.

She crawled over to Rayne and laid his head in her lap. He moaned and called her name, "Emerald. Somebody save Emerald and my baby." "Rayne," she cried, "your alive." "Thank God, you're alive. Just hold on baby. I'm right here. I love you so much. Please don't leave me," she pleaded. She rocked back and forth while holding his head. She heard the police at the door and rushed to open it. She immediately told them to get Rayne to the hospital as quickly as possible. They decided that after getting a police report they needed to take her to the hospital as well to make sure that she and the baby were ok from the trauma. Tony was unconscious but he wasn't dead.

She cried and cried as she rode in the ambulance with Rayne. He was hurt and it was all her fault. She should have never gotten involved with him. He stepped in front of a bullet for her. He saved her life. When they arrived at the hospital they found that Rayne was only grazed on his leg by the bullet. She never stopped to see where the blood came from when they were at the apartment. All of the excitement caused her to not be able to think straight. It never penetrated him and he would be fine. Emerald and the baby were fine too. However, the doctor asked her family to not allow her to deal with anything strenuous over the next few weeks to ensure that the baby would not be born prematurely.

When Emerald was released from the hospital she went to Rayne's room to check on him. "Hey handsome." "Hey Lady," he said and smiled while reaching out for her hands. "How are you?" "I'm ok. I'm just ready to get out of this hospital. The bullet didn't penetrate me so I don't see what the big deal is." "They just want to keep you here for observation that's all." Emerald's eyes began to water. Rayne eased up in the bed. "What's wrong baby? Why are you crying?" "I'm sorry I just keep seeing you lying on that floor and thinking about how I felt when thought I'd lost you." He pulled her down to kiss her forehead. "Well as you can see, I'm still here. I told you that I love you so much that I'd die for you." "You certainly did but I'm so glad that the mercy and grace of God covered you so that you could still be here with me and our baby."

"How's Tony?" Emerald's eyes sprang forth with water this time. "I don't know, he wasn't moving." "What? How? Did I shoot him?" "No, I hit him over the head too

many times with a vase. The one you gave me with the footprints poem written on it."
"He was knocked unconscious but he's definitely not dead. Emerald wiped her eyes. "The ambulance took him to the hospital and once he gets out he'll be in prison for a very long time."

"Rayne, if you weren't there I don't know what I would've done," Emerald sobbed. But God fixed it for me to be there. He pulled her to the bed so she could lie next to him. Now, I know it's going to be hard but lets put this day behind us. We've got a wedding to finish planning. He laid her head on his chest knowing that nothing could interrupt her life and God not have a way of escape for her.

The very next day, Rayne got an apartment across town and rented a moving truck. He would not have his wife and child living in a place where something so tragic happened.

CHAPTER 28

On the day before the wedding, Emerald's church family got together and threw a bridal and baby shower in one for her. She got tons of things for the baby. She got a stroller and car seat in one, two walkers, one jumper seat, playpen, crib and more clothes than the closet could hold. She was so happy. They played games and had a lovely time. There were moments that they laughed together and cried together too but it was all in love. The members of the Mt. New James We Fight for Our Own, Back in the Woods Church along with her family, were her strength.

Saturday came so fast but still not fast enough. It was the day that she'd say, "I do," to Rayne Washington. She woke up and felt so excited that she thought she'd jump out of her clothes. Tony almost stole this away from her but when the devil says no God still says yes. She showered and prepared herself some breakfast. While eating, the telephone rang. "Hello." "Hey Mrs. Washington," Rayne said. "Hey baby," Emerald said grinning from ear to ear. "Are you ready for our big day," Rayne asked? "Am I ready? Five O' Clock can't get her fast enough!" "Yeah, I feel the same way." "Rayne why do you sound so sad?" "I'm not sad actually. I'm just overwhelmed right now that God has answered my prayers. You're going to be my wife." She heard him sniff. "Rayne are you crying?" Emerald was shocked but laughed a little too. He was a big baby!

"No, I'm not crying. I've let you see me cry too many times already." Emerald laughed more. "Oh the little baby's crying," she said in a childlike voice. "I'm going to show you

who the little baby is tonight," Rayne said
teasingly. "Oh, ok, you're just feeling real
confident today aren't you?" "Yep." "I
love you, you know that Rayne?" "I love
you too baby," Rayne said. Emerald knew
that he meant it from his heart.

CHAPTER 29
The churchyard was once again packed even
though they'd invited only a few people.
However, those people invited other people
too. Emerald was fifteen minutes late. She
was so nervous. She gotten her shoulder
length hair spiral curled. Her wedding gown
had diamonds on various spots across her
chest. The sleeves were shear and see
through. The bottom flowed in a circular
motion down and pass her legs. Her train
followed behind her with a diamond pattern
on it as well. She did her own make up and
she looked absolutely stunning.

She entered the foyer area of the church and
heard the soloist singing. She peeked
through the door and saw Rayne standing
there. He looked incredibly handsome in his
tuxedo. Her mother did all of the
decorations and the church looked
completely different. From the windows
hung wife chiffon with gold glitter all over
it. A green and white bouquet of flowers sat
in the middle of each window. Gold and
white candles lit the entire building. The

bridesmaids marched in sage dresses with glass slippers. They wore silver accessories. All of a sudden Emerald heard a bell ringing. A little voice that belonged to Pamela's son, David yelled out, "The bride is coming, the bride is coming, the bride is coming," as he ran around the entire church. The keyboardist hit the key for the bride's entrance. The door opened and Emerald stepped back and to the side so she wouldn't be seen. She was crying so hard that her makeup was running. Her wedding directors tried to clean her face with Kleenex and preserve her make up.

She couldn't believe that this day was finally here. She was getting married. Out of all the hurt and pain that she'd been through with other men, she was finally marrying her Boaz. She got herself together and walked to the entrance of the sanctuary. The music began to play. She walked in accordance to the beat of the music. Her parents met her halfway down the isle. Both of them helped to make her so both of them should give her away. Her father stood on the left and her mother stood on the right. They each held one of her arms. "You look so beautiful her father whispered in her ear." "Oh, look at my baby," her mother said while trying to hold back tears. Just then Emerald felt the baby kick her. She looked down at her stomach for a brief moment, realizing that not only was she getting the best husband in the world but also the best father for her child.

Rayne met them at the altar. He kissed her mom on the cheek and shook her father's hand. "Thank you," Rayne said to them. He then took Emerald's hand and walked to Pastor Dudley. Pastor Dudley began the ceremony. Rayne and Emerald stated their vowels to one another.

"I Rayne Washington, take thee Emerald Sinclair, to be my lawfully wedded wife, to have and to hold from this day forward, till death to us part."

Emerald stated the same vowels to him. When Pastor Dudley said, "you may kiss the bride," Emerald turned and gave her flowers to Flora, her maid of honor. Flora kissed, hugged her and said congratulations. Rayne and Emerald then turned to each other. Rayne's face was wet with tears. She wiped his face with her hands, wrapped her arms around his neck and kissed him ever so passionately and sweetly. When the kiss was over she looked into his eyes and said, "I love you Rayne." He cried even harder. She held his hand and faced the audience as they announced, Mr. And Mrs. Rayne Washington. The sanctuary rang with applauds and cheers.

They left for the reception and had a marvelous time there. Emerald's cheeks hurt from smiling for so many pictures. After the reception they stayed at one of the five star hotels in Charleston. They decided not to go to far away in fear that Emerald would go into labor due to all of the excitement.

When they entered the room, the sound of jazz filled the room. Rose petals were all over the bed. Candles were setup and only needed to be lit. Rayne grabbed Emerald's hand and kissed them gently. "Why don't I go and get out of this gown and into something more appropriate for tonight's occasion," Emerald said in a seductive tone. Rayne said, "ok," and let her go. When she entered the bathroom, she noticed the Jacuzzi which was lined with candles. She filled the Jacuzzi with water and got in. Rose petals were in the bottom of the Jacuzzi so when she turned on the water they rose to the top. She poured in vanilla scented bubble bath.

"Rayne," she called out to him. He knocked on the door. "Are you ok," he asked still not entering the room? "No I'm not actually. Can you come in please?" "Are you sure?" "Oh I'm positive," Emerald answered with a relaxed look on her face.

Rayne opened the door and saw Emerald sitting in the Jacuzzi. She motioned with her finger for him to come in with her. "Emerald, if I come in there we might not make it to the bedroom." "That's fine with me," Emerald smiled. He undressed and Emerald's eyes widened more and more with every article of clothing he removed. "I'm going to be one happy lady," she thought to herself.

Rayne got some matches and lit the candles around the Jacuzzi and the rest is up to you, the reader, to figure out!

PART
4
WHAT HAPPENED TO EVERYONE?

CHAPTER 30

Weeks went by and Rayne and Emerald were very happy with each other. A few disagreements occurred but they always allowed it to be over before they went to sleep or left the other's presence.

One day Emerald was perming her sister, Janelle's hair again. Rayne watched them from a distance. When Janelle left he asked Emerald, "Why don't you go and get your Cosmetology license?" "I can't because I have to work." "Who told you that," Rayne asked while walking over to her? "No one told me that but Rayne I've worked all of my life. I would feel uncomfortable not clocking in and out everyday." "Baby you weren't created to clock in and out everyday. You're anointed for entrepreneurship. I'm your husband and it's my job and my pleasure to take care of you. Come and sit down Emerald." She sat next to him at the table. "After you deliver lil mama I want you to go back to school and get your license. We both know that it's your dream. Let's make it a reality."

"But Rayne." "No buts Emerald. Do you want to do hair Emerald? Yes or no?" "Yes but." "Then it's final." "No more BUT's or what ifs," Rayne said in an authoritative tone that excited Emerald.

"Ok honey," she said humbly. "But what about the baby, who will baby-sit?" "My mom is home everyday. She can keep the baby. She was going to talk to you anyway about baby-sitting for us while you worked." "Ok Daddy, whatever you say." Emerald kissed him on his lips.

CHAPTER 31

Two weeks later Emerald gave birth to a beautiful baby girl named Hannah Washington. Coincidentally, Hannah looks just like Rayne. Hair school has gone well and one year later, Emerald has her license and is working in a booming hair salon.

Rayne and Hannah can't be separated. She's a daddy's girl to her heart. As for Tony, he's still in jail for attempted kidnapping and murder. Hannah will be a grown woman before he gets out!

Emerald started a single's ministry in her church that reaches Christian women all over the world. The people in her community still act crazy at times but she gets preaching engagements all over the country where she ministers about the love of Christ and how essential it is to save your body for your husband.

Saturday came and after closing up the salon, Rayne, Emerald and 1 ½ year old Hannah decide to go get some ice cream and hit the beach. When they got there Rayne and Hannah ran and played in the water.

Emerald watched the waves as they floated towards them. She looked up at the sun and the clouds admiring how beautiful the scenery was. She thought to herself, "If I had aborted my baby, I would have missed out on all of this. I was single, pregnant and preaching but now I'm married, a mother and incredibly happy."

As far as Rayne was concerned, God kept his promise after all!

**WORDS OF MOTIVATION AND
ENCOURAGEMENT FROM THE
AUTHOR OF SINGLE, PREGNANT
AND PREACHING.**

I hope that this book has given you the capability of better understanding God's grace and mercy in our lives. The word of God says, "For all have sinned and come short of the glory of God" (KJV Romans 3:23). There is no perfect boy, girl, man or woman on this earth. It doesn't matter if you are an Apostle, a pugh member or someone in between, you have and you will make mistakes. However, we must remember that God loves us so much. His love for us is unconditional. You may have made a mistake like Emerald or something further than that but just like Emerald, you must sincerely repent and sin no more.

There is a difference between an intentional sin and an unintentional sin. When your phone rings and it's after 9 pm, that man does not want to come over just to talk! What is his motive and what it yours also? We must not yield into temptation. There are some sins that we willfully walk into. We must make a conscious decision to do everything in our power not to fulfill the lust of the flesh. We must love God and love his will more than we love our will or ourselves!

We must also decide not to repeat our sins over and over again. People tend to abuse the fact that God's grace is sufficient but trust me; you don't want to fall into the hands of an angry God! We must be completely delivered from our sins. We must lay aside the sin that causes us to get off track with God.

Sin separates us from God! Don't commit spiritual adultery by cheating on God! How do you cheat on God you ask? You cheat on God by fulfilling the lust of the flesh, by being disobedient to the voice of the Lord, and obeying the voice of satan. How do you obey the voice of satan? You obey the voice of satan by doing what you know is wrong. Then you come back and say, "Lord, I'm sorry." But the question is, do you really mean it? Now you have to work to get back to where you were in God before the sin took place.

Listen, I understand that you are human but you have Christ, the greater one, living on the inside of you. I tried to write this book to attract the audience of single women. Married women have struggles and I have a book on the way for you. However, singles have struggles too. It doesn't matter how much you speak in tongues, or run around the church and dance, you will have struggles. You still live in a body and your body craves love, attention and if we can just be real—it craves sex. However, my sisters, "greater is he that is in you than he that is in the world" (KJV I John 4:4). You are stronger than your desire! Sex does not have a hold on you because you walk in the power and the anointing of God. You can survive. Sisters, you have the power over the enemy and he is defeated in every area of your life. Don't relinquish that power and victory by allowing sin to get in the way.

Ladies, if you are involved with someone like the character of Tony then by all means, get out! Run fast. Run for your life. Tony came and went as he pleased because the character, Emerald let him. He was fine. He looked like what she wanted. But he was a wolf in sheep clothing. Ladies you deserve to be loved. You deserve to be happy and shown attention. You deserve a man of God. To make it plainer,You deserve more than what you want! I speak to your insecurities and command you to have security in God. You are beautiful, intelligent and anointed.

If you are in sin, come out of it. Stop fornicating. Leave that married man alone. Leave that separated man alone. He's still married if those divorce papers have not been finalized. If he can't wait on those papers then you really don't need to be with him. A man with integrity would want to do things the right way. Stop shacking up! If

he can live with you then he can surely
marry you! You ARE good enough to
marry. Your relationship with God is on the
line. If you don't wake up on tomorrow
where will you spend eternity, heaven or
hell? If you're fornicating, committing
adultery, shacking, etc., then hell will be
your answer and your home.

There are a few more things that I want to
touch on. One of them is masturbation. So
you're not sleeping with Tony but when you
masturbate, the person or thing that you
fantasize about is who you're sleeping with.
Let me answer all of you who ask is
masturbation a sin or is masturbation wrong.
The answer is yes and yes again. It's wrong
because you are lusting in your mind and
acting it out in the flesh. Is lusting a sin?
Yes, it is a sin. (Read II Corinthians 10:5.)

Another thing that I want to talk about is
dating relationships. Is it all right to
date/marry a man whom is not saved? The
answer is no! How can two walk together
unless they agree? What I'm about to say
will seem harsh but it's the truth. You are
serving God and they are serving satan. "A
friend of the world is an enemy of God"
(KJV James 4:4). You should be in
agreeance about salvation and you both
should be living a life of sanctification. If
you've already married him then that's a

done deal. The bible says that a sanctified wife makes a sanctified husband. It didn't say anything about a girlfriend. Don't walk open eyed off of a cliff! If you're single remember that your husband should be the priest of the home. He should be led by the spirit of Christ. If he is not saved then whom is he being led by? Now, in retrospect, I know that some of you may end dating an unsaved man. Here's my advise to you, IF YOU ARE NOT STRONG ENOUGH TO LEAD HIM TO CHRIST then leave him alone. If you don't, you will FALL into temptation.

I know that you have tons of questions for God. Some of them maybe, why am I not married? When am I getting married? Where is my husband? When will I meet him, etc.? Please understand however, that sin hides these answers from you. Sin causes you to not receive answers and blessings from God. Where there is no repentance there is no revelation. Your husband can't spot you out because when he sees you he also sees sin! This is not the answer for everyone because some of you are living upright before the Lord. You are simply in a position of standing still.

However, if you are in sin, clean yourself up! Don't walk into Emerald's shoes. It only took one night and one time for

Emerald to mess up and a seed was planted. That seed was Hannah, which is a beautiful thing but Hannah should have been planted after Emerald said, "I do."

If you are Emerald and you're still single then wait on God! Don't marry your baby's daddy just because that's who he is. If you marry him then do it because that's what God said to do. Hear the voice of God and not of your Flesh! And remember, if you're like Emerald then you're still single and you're pregnant or you have a child. Don't make the mistake of having sex outside of wedlock again. Trust me, you can wait! You're only using sex as a way to feel loved anyway!

God is the greatest lover and the greatest power! Who can love you like Jesus? NOBODY! I have experienced the hand of God hold me when I was single and even now that I'm married. It's better than anything that you could experience with a man.

God's love is better than the feel of any man on any given day! Enter into the presence of the almighty God, Our Lord and Savior Jesus Christ. Learn to love on him. Let him be your husband you be his bride. You are royalty. You are a jewel to the man that he has for you and you should be cherished.

Wait on him. Let him find you as the words says. Keep sin out of your life so that when you go out, your husband will be able to see you and not a blanket of sin covering you. Be clothed with a garment of praise, power and the character of Christ.

I love you my sisters,

Prophetess Melvina Carpenter,
Elder of True Light Healing and Deliverance Ministries
107 St. James Ave. Ste B1
Goose Creek, SC 29455
FIND ME ON YOUTUBE.COM

***All references are from the King James Version of the Holy Bible unless otherwise noted.

45271757R00094

Made in the USA
Charleston, SC
15 August 2015